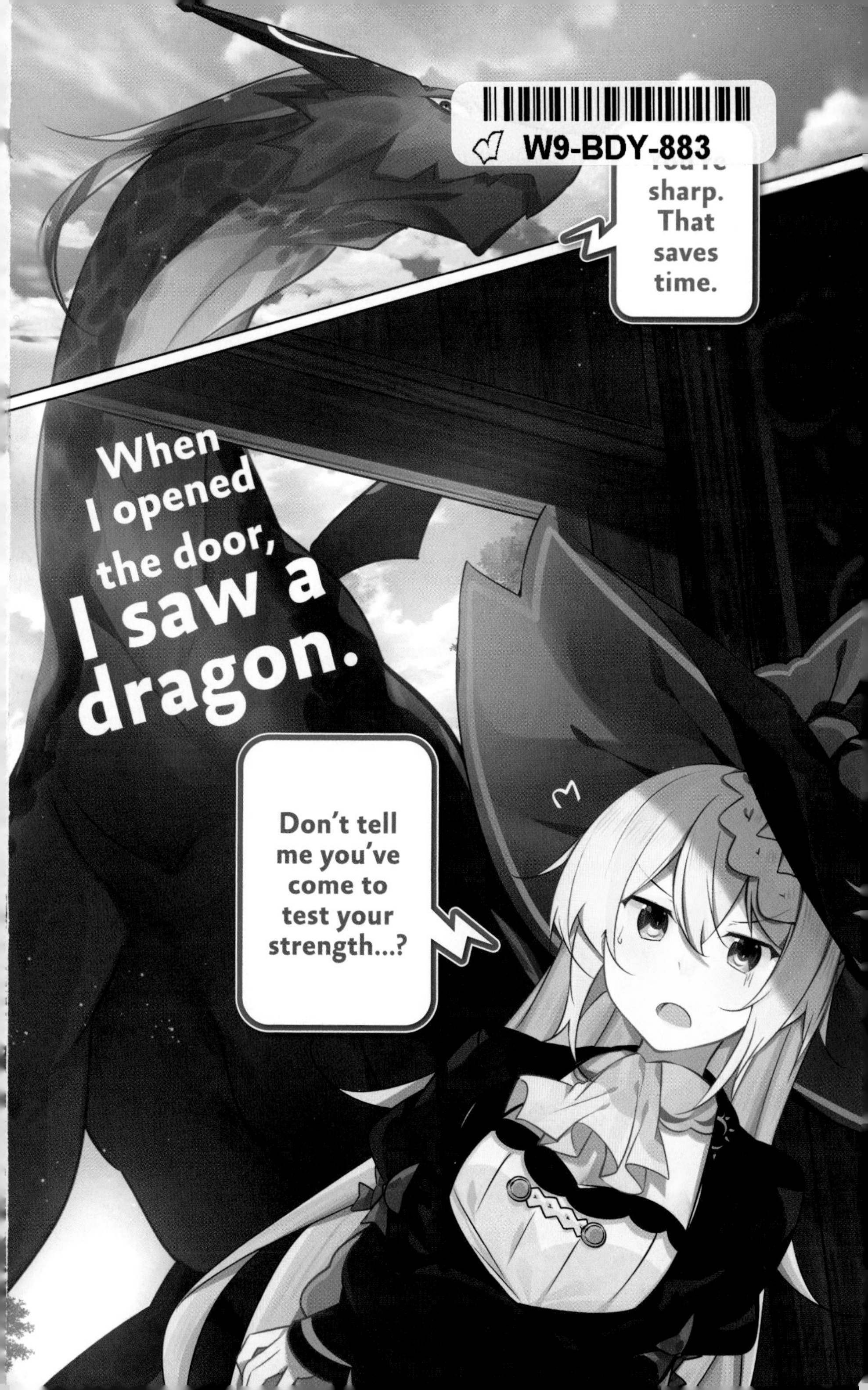
sharp. That saves time.
When I opened the door, I saw a dragon.
Don't tell me you've come to test your strength...?

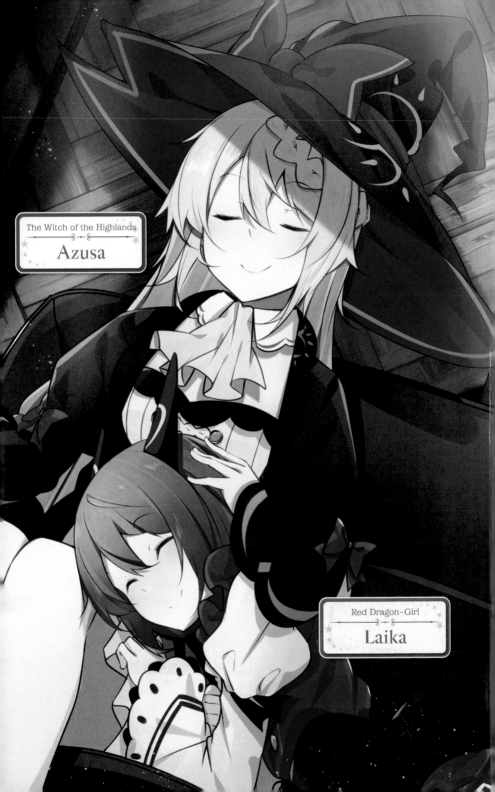

The Witch of the Highlands
**Azusa**

Red Dragon-Girl
**Laika**

Slime Spirit (Little Sister)
**Shalsha**

Elf Apothecary
**Halkara**

Slime Spirit (Big Sister)
**Falfa**

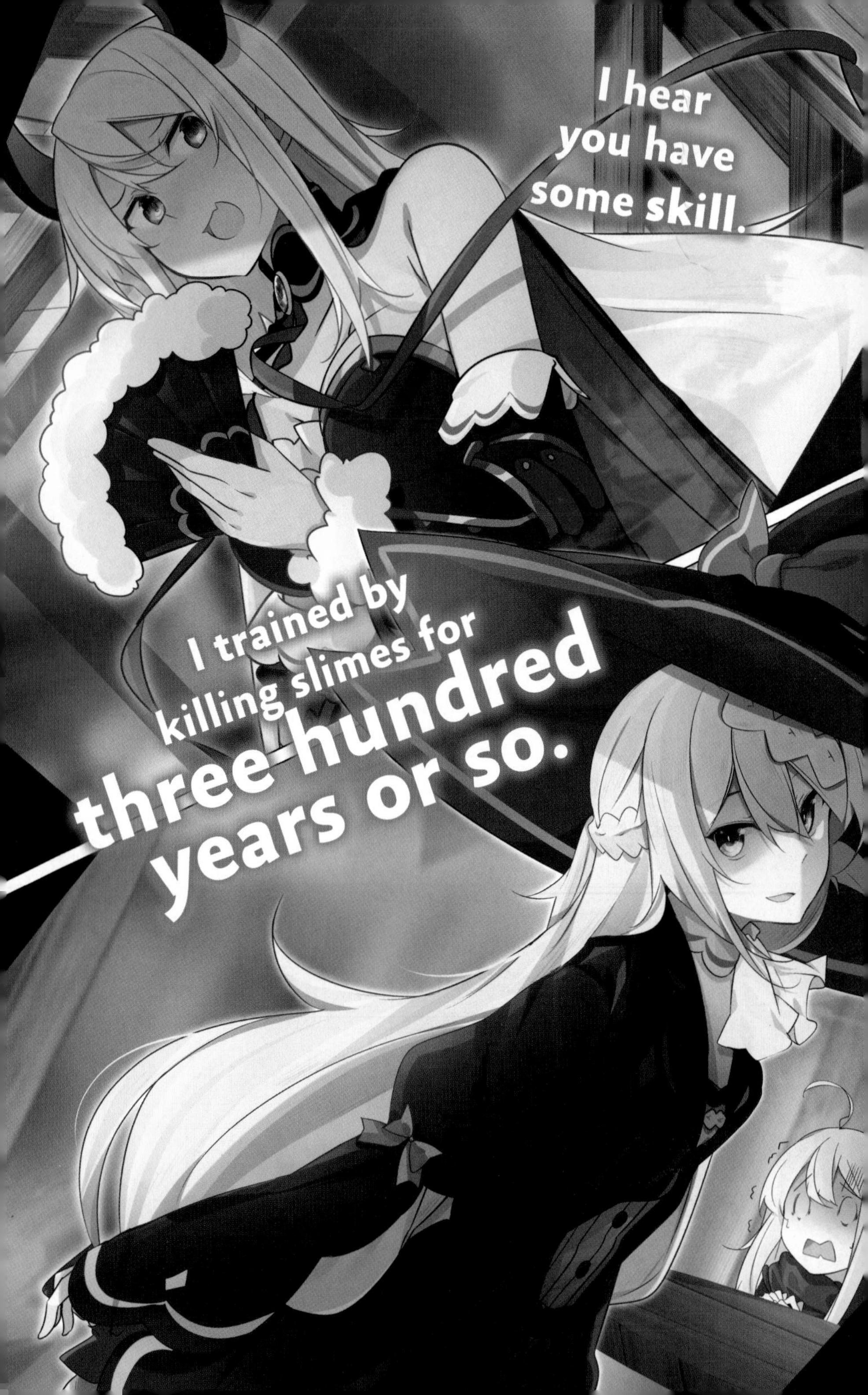
I hear you have some skill.
I trained by killing slimes for three hundred years or so.

# I've Been Killing SLIMES for 300 Years and Maxed Out My Level 1

KISETSU MORITA

Translation by Taylor Engel
Cover art by Benio

This book is a work of fiction. Names, characters, places, and incidents are the product of the author's imagination or are used fictitiously. Any resemblance to actual events, locales, or persons, living or dead, is coincidental.

SLIME TAOSHII E SANBYAKUNEN, SHIRANAIUCHINI
LEVEL MAX NI NATTEMASHITA vol. 1
Copyright © 2017 Kisetsu Morita
Illustrations copyright © 2017 Benio
All rights reserved.
Original Japanese edition published in 2017 by SB Creative Corp.

This English edition is published by arrangement with SB Creative Corp., Tokyo in care of Tuttle-Mori Agency, Inc., Tokyo.

English translation © 2018 by Yen Press, LLC

Yen On
1290 Avenue of the Americas
New York, NY 10104

Visit us at yenpress.com
facebook.com/yenpress
twitter.com/yenpress
yenpress.tumblr.com
instagram.com/yenpress

First Yen On Edition: April 2018

Yen On is an imprint of Yen Press, LLC.
The Yen On name and logo are trademarks of Yen Press, LLC.

The publisher is not responsible for websites (or their content) that are not owned by the publisher.

Library of Congress Cataloging-in-Publication Data
Names: Morita, Kisetsu, author. | Benio, illustrator. | Engel, Taylor, translator.
Title: I've been killing slimes for 300 years and maxed out my level/ Kisetsu Morita ;
illustration by Benio ; translation by Taylor Engel.
Other titles: Slime taoshite sanbyakunen, shiranaiuchini level max ni nattemashita. English |
I have been killing slimes for 300 years
Description: First Yen On edition. | New York : Yen On, 2018–
Identifiers: LCCN 2017059843 | ISBN 9780316448277 (v. 1 : paperback)
Subjects: | CYAC: Reincarnation—Fiction. | Witches—Fiction.
Classification: LCC PZ7.1.M6725 Iv 2018 | DDC [Fic]—dc23
LC record available at https://lccn.loc.gov/2017059843

ISBNs: 978-0-316-44827-7 (paperback)
978-0-316-44828-4 (ebook)

1 3 5 7 9 10 8 6 4 2

LSC-C

Printed in the United States of America

# Contents

Story by Kisetsu Morita Illustration by Benio

She slaughtered slimes for 300 years...

Azusa Aizawa, twenty-seven, female, single.

Corporate wage slave.

I lived for my job and only for my job.

I set aside romance, leisure, and everything else for the daily slog.

My record was fifty consecutive work days. I wonder what happened to the Labor Standards Act...

One day, while I was working away, I blacked out.

When I opened my eyes again, I saw the face of a young woman. She appeared to have angel wings, or something like them.

"Oh. I died, didn't I...?"

In the end, my life had been empty of everything except punching the clock.

I didn't know whether this individual was an angel or a grim reaper, but she was probably something along those lines.

"That's right. You worked too much, and it killed you in your twenties. You poor thing..."

The girl pitied me. She must have been a kind person.

"Though this could never truly make up for it, I will ensure that your next life has the potential to bring you sheer happiness. What sort of power would you like? If you wish, you could be reborn as a royal princess. Oh, and either gender is fine. You are free to choose nearly anything."

"I can wish for anything? Really?"

"Yes! I have a habit of indulging women, you see."

*Isn't that gender inequality? Well, I suppose I'd rather have fewer restrictions than more.*

"Make me completely immortal, then, if you would."

That was what I wished for.

Work had run me ragged until the end of a short life, so for this round, I wanted to take my time.

"In that case, I'll reincarnate you in a body that circulates mana so you won't age."

Evidently, she could just do things like that. Fantastic.

"Do you have any other requests?"

"No, that's enough for me."

"You're sure?"

"Yes. What I want is a long, slow, laid-back life. I'd like to be self-sufficient for the basics and live up in the mountains or somewhere similar. Then, if I could help out in a nearby village in exchange for things like salt that are harder to come by, I'm not sure I could ask for more."

I'd lived in metropolitan Tokyo, so I wanted a carefree existence in a house in the mountains. Granted, all I'd seen of that metropolis was the route between my apartment and my office, so I couldn't exactly claim to have had my fill of big-city life, but still.

"I can see how hard your former life must have been. All right. I'll give you a fresh start with eternal youth in the peaceful highlands. I'm sure you didn't intend to request a long life as an old lady, so let's make you immortal at seventeen."

My consciousness faded out again.

When I awoke, I was lying on a high plain.

There was a single house nearby.

As I approached, I noticed a sign posted on the door.

Interestingly enough, although it couldn't have been in Japanese, I could somehow read it.

> This has been our house for a long time, but we're going to move in with our son and his wife, who live in town. If anyone wants it, they're welcome to it. We've left the door unlocked.

"What incredibly generous people. Luck is really on my side. No, I suppose it isn't really luck. That angel-girl did reincarnate me here on purpose."

Speaking of reincarnation, I wondered what I looked like now. I went into the house and hunted for a mirror.

"I'm seventeen, all right. Not a bad face. The European features will take some getting used to, but still."

I had stunning blond hair that fell to my waist, and my eyes were a vivid light blue, almost turquoise. I didn't know how beauty was measured in this world, but I was pretty cute. If I decided to go to high school, I'd probably get all the boys.

I wasn't wearing the white clothes of the dead, either. These were straight out of a fantasy world, complete with a pointy black hat that would be unmistakable even from a distance. It looked vaguely witchy.

"Okay. Starting today, this is my house. Azusa's house!"

I was in another world now, and I thought katakana script might fit the atmosphere better than the standard kanji character I'd always used to write my name. It would also help it sink in that I'd turned over a new leaf. That settled it: I'd start calling myself "Azusa" in katakana.

There was a plowed field beside the house that I'd most likely be able to harvest vegetables from. If I wanted a self-sufficient life, this place was ready-made for it.

There were fifteen or so gold coins in the clothes I'd been reincarnated in, so buying the bare necessities was unlikely to present a problem.

A knife hung at my waist as well. I was a woman living alone, so it was probably wise to have something like this.

At the bottom of the hill, I saw a small town. More of a village, really.

"Maybe I'll wander over and do a little shopping."

I wanted to ask about the area anyway.

On the way to the village, my path was blocked by a jiggly, jellylike creature.

"Oh. A slime?"

Maybe it was the thing's appearance, but I wasn't worried at all. A cat might as well have stepped out in front of me. That said, like any monster, it clearly meant to attack me. With cats, the mere sight of a human was generally enough to give them a start and make them back off, so the situations weren't exactly the same.

I drew my knife. If this was a slime, I had to kill it.

I attacked.

The knife slid into the gelatinous body.

*Blorp!* A weird sensation traveled through my hand to the rest of me.

Had that done anything...? Well, I'd stabbed it, so I'd probably inflicted damage.

Round two.

*Blorp!*

That one had more of an effect, maybe.

The angry (I assumed) slime rammed me. The impact knocked me back a step, but it didn't really hurt.

Safe in the knowledge I wouldn't be harmed, I went after it mercilessly.

"Take that, and that, and that!"

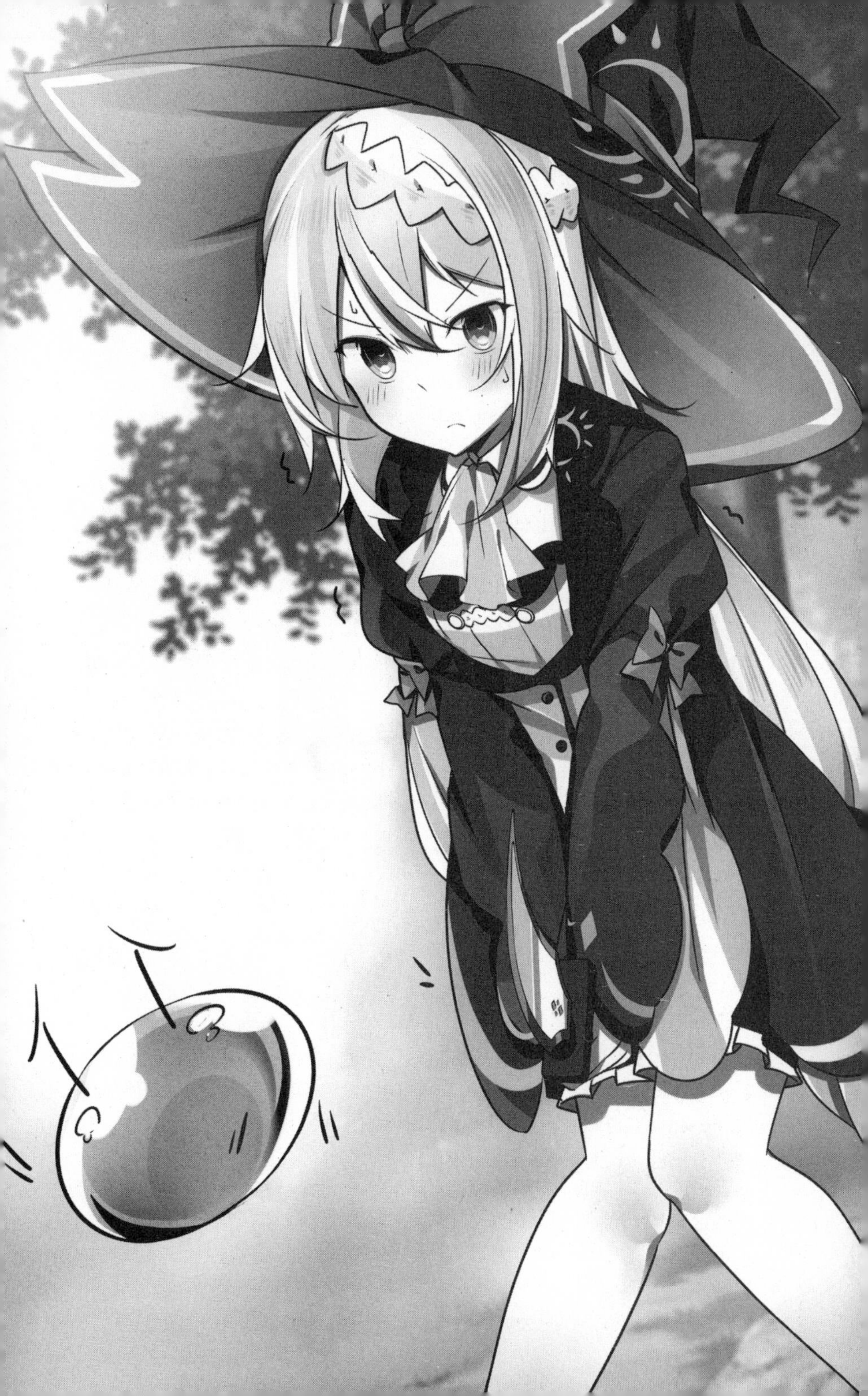

One of those blows must have finished it off, as the slime changed shape and became a small jewel.

In games, when you kill monsters, you get money. This probably served that purpose.

Self-sufficient though I might have been, I'd need currency to buy daily necessities, so I took it without hesitation.

Before I reached the village, I encountered and killed two more slimes.

*Slimes seem to be pretty common.*

The village wasn't that big, but it was trim and tidy. It looked rather Swiss.

Come to think of it, sightseeing in Switzerland had been a dream of mine, but in the end, I worked myself to death and had never gotten to do it.

Well, even if I'd had vacation time, I probably would have spent it at home sleeping as much as I possibly could instead of going on a trip.

I spotted a kind-looking woman and called to her.

"Excuse me. I've just moved into a house in the highlands. Could you tell me about this village?"

"This is the village of Flatta. I'd say young Natalie at Guild Reception is quite knowledgeable about the place. She introduces it to adventurers who journey here from other areas, so she's used to explaining things."

*I see. Makes sense.*

"Thank you very much."

"This is your first time visiting, isn't it? I'll take you to the guild. Though, it's a small village, so I imagine you'd find it on your own before too long."

"Great, thanks!"

I followed the woman—who actually was as kind as she'd looked—to the guild. It was indeed small. This place was peaceful enough, and there probably wasn't a need for many adventurers around these parts.

"Oh, Mrs. Imal, good afternoon."

"Natalie, this girl is our new neighbor. Tell her about the village, would you?"

"Yes, of course. I'll go over it with you right here at reception."

Mrs. Imal left us then. She lived nearby, so we'd probably run into each other again soon.

"I'm Azusa. I moved into the house in the highlands."

"Oh, there? It's a nice place, but not so convenient for the elderly. It'll be ideal to have someone young living there."

Then Natalie gave me the rundown about this little hamlet.

Maybe because she'd explained the same things many, many times before, her spiel was smooth and practiced.

First and foremost, she said, the village was peaceful, tranquil, and serene. Even on a casual stroll you could sense the clearly pastoral atmosphere. Cows and sheep were in no short supply, and if the area had a local specialty, it was their dairy products.

The count who owned this land lived far away, and the village chief he'd appointed was a native with a drama-free regime.

"Slimes are just about the only monsters around here. As a result, it's so safe that you could even nap outside the village."

"Excellent."

"It's a small community, but you'll be able to buy the basic everyday staples—bread and salt and things—so don't worry. However, with our low population, trading may prove difficult."

What Natalie said reminded me of something.

"Oh yeah, so on the way here, I defeated a few slimes and ended up with these jewels. What are they?"

"Ah, when you kill a monster, you receive a gem known as a magic stone. You can exchange them for money here at the guild. These are worth six hundred gold—meaning six copper coins."

In Japanese currency, would that be about six hundred yen? That wouldn't cover more than a single trip to a café, but if rent was a non-issue, I'd be able to make a living killing only as many slimes as I needed.

"Okay, exchange them for me right away, please."

"To do that, you'll need to register with the guild as an adventurer. Is that all right?"

"Sure, no problem."

At that point, Natalie brought out an object that looked like a slate.

"First, place your hand on this slate, please. It'll display your class and status, and then we'll register that information at the guild."

I set my hand on it, mentally commenting that this reminded me of fingerprint authentication.

My status popped up in the upper part of the tablet.

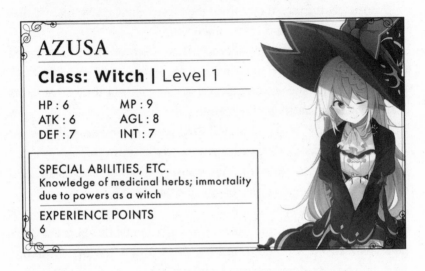

## AZUSA

### Class: Witch | Level 1

HP : 6  MP : 9
ATK : 6  AGL : 8
DEF : 7  INT : 7

SPECIAL ABILITIES, ETC.
Knowledge of medicinal herbs; immortality
due to powers as a witch

EXPERIENCE POINTS
6

"Whoa! You're immortal! That's incredible!"

Natalie was startled. Well, I guess you would be. My class was "witch," apparently.

"It's true that some witches can fine-tune the circulation of mana—er, magical power—in their bodies to extend their lives, but immortal at level 1… How can that be? You must have a tremendous aptitude for it."

"It sure is strange… Maybe I'm just lucky."

*I'll keep the stuff about the reincarnation bonus to myself.*

"Here, let me pay you for those magic stones."

She gave me six coppers.

"I'll start saving up by killing slimes, then."

"Yes, and the guild is looking forward to your patronage, Miss Azusa!"

I'd gotten some gold coins when I reincarnated, so I spent them on groceries and seeds to plant in my field.

Looked like I was all set to live here for a while.

Three more slimes showed up on my way home, so I vanquished them with my knife.

More magic stones and more of the money they would bring me.

After that day, my laid-back life began.

I did virtually nothing, day in and day out.

First, I slept as long as I wanted. I tended the field here and there. When I wanted some exercise, I killed slimes. Since they were a valuable source of cash, I made sure to dispatch at least twenty of them daily.

Sometimes I ventured into the nearby woods.

Maybe it was my status as a witch that let me immediately identify which plants were medicinal herbs. From time to time, I blended them into various concoctions and took them down to the village to sell. I wasn't trying to turn a profit, so I priced them at less than the market value.

When people in the village were suddenly taken ill, I'd examine them and give them my homemade herbal medicines. After all, I couldn't just stand by and watch the villagers drop like flies.

Thanks to that, people started calling me "the great Witch of the Highlands" out of respect.

Some of them even brought gifts like cheese and other dairy products up to the house. That was much appreciated.

I considered reading grimoires in my spare time, but they were really expensive! Still, after mowing down slimes for a while, I'd saved enough to buy several! Once I set my sights on something I wanted, slime slaying lit a fire in me.

Other than that…nothing unusual happened.

Possibly because I was immortal, I didn't age (of course), and I almost never got sick.

As a rule, no one came to see me at my house in the highlands which didn't trouble me much. I'd lived alone when I was an office worker in Japan, too.

It was during my second life that I first came to understand the meaning of "leisure with dignity," for sure.

And three hundred years passed.

You heard that right: I made a living by killing slimes for three hundred years.

When it came to defeating the little blobs, I had a fair bit of confidence.

I knew exactly where to stab them with my knife to finish them on the first attack.

Frankly, I could kill them unarmed with my bare hands or my feet. I could kill them with a forehead flick. I figured my level had probably gone up a bit.

Well, one day, I knocked on the door of the guild, as I always did. I needed to exchange my magic stones.

I took my spoils to the female staff member, who was a descendant of Natalie's, several generations removed. She'd started working here only recently, and I didn't know her name yet.

"Good afternoon."

"Oh, great Witch of the Highlands!"

By now, everyone knew me as "the Witch of the Highlands."

Having been alive for three centuries, I was the most knowledgeable about the village's history.

"Here are today's magic stones. Twenty-six slimes' worth."

"Yes, indeed they are. That's fifty-two hundred gold, then."

I put the money in my leather bag.

"Oh, that's right. Great Witch of the Highlands, there's something I've been wondering about."

"Hmm? What's up?"

"How strong are you, exactly?"

"Strong? In combat, you mean? I don't know, or, well, I doubt it's anything impressive."

I'd registered as an adventurer so I could get money for magic stones, but I'd never actually adventured. After all, adventuring meant risking your life. A leisurely, peaceful life suited me better.

The employee brought out the old slate.

"Um, would it be all right if I checked your status?"

"My status? You know, I don't think I've seen it at all in the past three hundred years."

I hadn't needed to. In this area, *monster* just meant *slime*. I'd never actually sensed that I was leveling up, either.

That said, claiming that I'd only ever fought slimes would be a lie.

In the forest, there were horned rabbits. Big caterpillars, too. Those monsters were still weak, though, and my knife brought me easy victories.

That knife might have been specially made. I'd been using it for three centuries at this point, and there were still no nicks in the blade.

If you actually gave it some thought, that was astonishing. This thing could be worth a fortune. Not that I'd sell an item that had taken such good care of me for thirty decades.

"You've watched over Flatta for so long, great Witch of the Highlands! I believe your status is probably astronomical as a result. I want to know what it is, so…!"

The young staff member's eyes were brimming with fervent expectation.

It's embarrassing to say this myself, but the people of Flatta respected me.

True, I gave them a hand whenever the village was in trouble. Over the centuries, several plagues had swept through, and every time, I'd whipped up herbal curatives in bulk, created strengthening tinctures, and worked hard to ensure there were no deaths.

In addition, as I'd watched over the village from the highlands since before its current inhabitants were born, they seemed to view me as some sort of guardian deity.

As far as I was concerned, I was simply enjoying my life of R & R, which made that reverence feel excessive and uncomfortable.

"I don't mind if you check my status, but I'm just a long-lived witch who knows a thing or two about herbalism. I hope you're not expecting it to look like some legendary adventurer's."

"Oh, you're too modest. It may not seem impressive to you, but you're judging by your own standards, aren't you?"

"Well, go ahead and look. It's going to be normal."

I put my hand on the slate.

If this had been Japan, the environment would probably have changed drastically over three hundred years, but changes in this world were small. The slate was still functional and in use. Well, its ability to display statuses felt high tech to me, but anyway.

**AZUSA**

**Class: Witch | Level 99**

HP : 533     MP : 867
ATK : 468    AGL : 841
DEF : 580    INT : 953

MAGIC
Teleportation, Levitation, Flame, Whirlwind, Item Appraisal, Earthquake, Ice and Snow, Lightning Attack, Mind Control, Break Spell, Detoxify, Reflect Spell, Mana Absorption, Language Comprehension, Transformation, Spell Creation

SPECIAL ABILITIES, ETC.
Knowledge of medicinal herbs; immortality due to powers as a witch; EXP acquisition boost

EXPERIENCE POINTS
10,840,086

"……Huh?"

*Now, that's a strange number…*

"Uh, you know, I bet the slate's broken. I mean, it's saying 'level 99,' so…"

"Aaaaaaaaaaaaaaaaaaaaaaaah!!! Great Witch, you're way, way too strooooooooong!!!!!!!" The receptionist was so shocked I thought she might collapse. "That's insane! You have to be the strongest in the world!"

"I'm telling you, that rock's broken. All I've fought are slimes, you know? How could I actually have almost eleven million experience points?"

"Let's see… You've killed slimes for three hundred years, three hundred sixty-five days a year, without skipping a day, correct? Of course, I don't know about what happened long ago, so I'm extrapolating from what I've heard from the village elders, but…"

Incidentally, this world has a proper sun and moon and uses a solar calendar.

"That sounds about right. I think it's been twenty-five slimes or so per day, on average. When I wanted to buy a grimoire or make repairs on the house or something like that, I remember going all out and plowing through a whole bunch to earn money."

As you'd expect, after decades upon decades, the house in the mountains had been remodeled so much that it had practically been rebuilt.

"Somewhere along the way, you also picked up a special ability that increases the number of experience points you acquire. From what I hear, you haven't traveled anywhere far away, so I think you probably got it at one of your level-ups."

"I suppose that could be."

Even if all I'd done was kill slime after slime, that bonus had probably boosted my level at least a little.

"That special ability increases the number of experience points you get per monster by two."

"What, just two?"

"Well, each slime normally gives two points, so it basically doubled. And now we'll calculate…

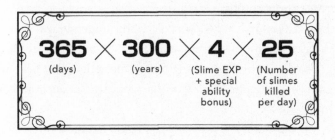

$$365 \times 300 \times 4 \times 25$$

(days) (years) (Slime EXP + special ability bonus) (Number of slimes killed per day)

I think the equation would look something like that."

"Yes, I'm following. Well, I wouldn't have had the EXP boost from the very beginning, so this number will probably be a little high, but still…"

The twenty-five-a-day figure was a rough estimate, and if it had been more than that, the total would be higher. It wasn't as though I'd never killed a non-slime monster, either.

"At any rate, I'll try running a calculation with this. Ten, nine, five, zero, zero, zero, zero… Let's see, how many thousands is that? …10,950,000!"

*That's pretty close to my 10,840,000!*

"Just so you know, large dragons are said to be worth 2,500 points, so 10,840,000 is enough for 4,380 of them."

"A dragon slayer extraordinaire!"

"It's the same as if you'd killed fourteen point six dragons per year…"

After putting it in dragon terms, I began to suspect I'd done something extraordinary.

"This figure isn't a slate error. I knew it! Great Witch of the Highlands, you really are a mighty and powerful witch!"

I was stunned. I couldn't believe that number.

I had sensed, intuitively, that I was growing.

After all, my physical body stayed seventeen, and only my experience grew.

That said, to think it would reach such a ludicrous number…

No. More importantly…

…there'd be trouble if I couldn't keep this under wraps.

They say that slow and steady wins the race, but this was too much winning. People might start asking for far more than just help around the village. For example: "A dragon has appeared at such-and-such a place. Go slay it."

I wouldn't mind, if it was just once. I could handle a single dragon.

However, if I did it even one time, I'd have no choice but to go slay dragons elsewhere. They'd be like, "You killed their dragon; why can't you kill ours?"

And if that happened, I could kiss my laid-back life good-bye.

My days would be filled with adventure, packed with hard labor from morning till night. In the end, I'd work myself to death.

Not that. Anything but that…

I'd have to keep the rumors from spreading.

"Um, miss, could you remind me of your name?"

"It's Natalie."

*What, Natalie?! Impossible! Is she immortal, too? —Probably not.*

The name wasn't super-unique. The two just happened to share it, that's all.

The name *Masayuki* was used during Japan's Warring States period, and it's still around in the current Heisei era, too.

"Natalie, keep this just between us, please. After all, a status is like a personal secret. You wouldn't want people gossiping about your bust size, would you?"

"I'm fairly secure in my bust size."

*Show-off.*

*Shoot, so she doesn't have a complex about her bust… She's definitely bigger than I am. Leveling up doesn't seem to change your cup size, and my figure's been the same for three hundred years.*

*Let's stop talking about this…*

"In any case, don't tell anyone about my status. That's all right, isn't it?"

"I understand. I'll take care not to let word get out that you're the most powerful of all, great Witch! I'd love to sing your praises to everyone, but as a resident of this village, I would never betray you!"

The prestige of the highland witch came through for me.

*Good, very good. If I can get her to stay quiet, this'll all work out.*

In three hundred years, the only one who'd ever taken an interest in my status was this woman, Natalie.

In other words, my peaceful days could very well last for another several centuries! Yeah, let's do that!

Relieved, I returned to my house in the highlands. To test whether that status was real, I used an Ice and Snow spell on a waterfall in the forest.

I still didn't believe it. After all, I'd felt almost nothing to suggest I'd gotten stronger.

"Freeze everything! Hiyaaah!"

The waterfall froze solid.

"Guess you could call that 'solid' proof…"

For a few days after that, I lazed around the house reading grimoires I'd bought a long time ago.

On a side note, I cooked in large batches, freezing most of it with my Ice and Snow magic, which I hadn't even realized I'd learned. To thaw out my food, I used Flame magic. I adapted that to use as fire in the kitchen, too. In a single bound, my magic raised my standard of living to the equivalent of modern society on Earth.

Which meant I was now able to spend all day lounging and dawdling around.

*Leveling up is the best!*

At this point, I could say this was real luxury, the true pleasure of living.

During my days as a corporate wage slave, going home on time had been like an urban legend. Even so-called holidays had often been consumed by work that came in the day before or by having so much to do in the first place that I was forced to go to the office in an attempt to catch up.

*Honestly, I don't care to do that ever again. I am hell-bent on my loafing.*

*That said, I have a whole lot of the same food frozen, and I do get tired of it.*

"Maybe I'll go to a restaurant in the village and eat out. It's been a while."

I headed down to Flatta.

I had spells that probably would have gotten me there easily, like Levitation and Teleportation, but I was afraid that if people saw those, they'd figure out that my level was high. So I walked. It's better for your figure anyway.

On the way, as expected, I encountered a slime.

*So three hundred years isn't enough time for slimes to evolve?* I thought, flicking it with a finger.

That was all it took to end the slime's life. Come to think of it, my knife had eventually become too bothersome, so for the most part, I'd taken to smacking them to death.

Was that also because I had unwittingly raised my attack power?

*Still*, I thought, *witches have pretty strong physical attacks, too.*

Even if my level was high, I was conscientious about picking up the magic stones the slimes generated. I had no other source of income. I wasn't hurting for money, but if something was there for the taking, I wouldn't pass it up.

After killing several slimes, I reached the village. The way there was downhill, which made it nice and easy.

I entered a restaurant called the Savvy Eagle.

This place had good omelets. They kept lots of chickens at the shop, and the eggs were fresh.

"It's been a while. It's me, Azusa."

"Well, if it isn't the great Witch of the Highlands!"

I greeted the restaurant's owner, who was in charge of the cooking.

When I sat down in my normal seat, the proprietress brought me my usual drink before I even ordered it. My body was seventeen, but yes, I drank alcohol. After all, I'd lived in this world for three centuries.

"Here you go, great Witch. One stiff drink."

"Thank you much. I think I'll have an omelet again today. Oh, and bring some beef stew as well, please."

"Yes, great Witch."

It's nice to be a regular.

When I was an office worker, I had been under too much stress to check out new restaurants. At lunchtime, all the places were jam-packed with customers, and I wasn't able to take my time. As a rule, I ate extremely unfeminine meals, like convenience store bentos and instant ramen.

Before long, my omelet arrived.

You could tell it was a masterpiece just by looking. I totally would have Instagrammed it.

It was faintly sweet from the first bite. Truly delicious.

"Your omelets are the best in the world, aren't they?"

"Your long life has earned you some skill with your compliments, great Witch. Have you ever actually gone to another town and tried their omelets?"

"They're the best in my world, and that's good enough for me!"

"True, of all our customers, I think you're the one who savors them the most."

The proprietress and I have been bantering like this for over fifteen years, so we're seasoned experts.

"Oh, by the way, great Witch, there was something I wanted to ask you," the woman said.

"Yes? What is it?"

"Is it true you're level 99?"

The light faded from my eyes.

"Huh? Where in the world did you hear such a completely unfounded rumor?"

There was nothing for it but to play dumb. If I acted shocked, it would come back to bite me later.

"I don't really know where it started, but that's what I heard. The neighborhood children were talking about it."

So where had the children heard it?

Actually, it was too late. This wasn't a big village, and I was the closest thing to a celebrity around here, so there was a good possibility the story had gotten out.

*I'll have to give Natalie a talking-to later. What's done is done, but I'll make her think long and hard about breaking her promises.*

Well, unless I showed them my magic, no one could prove my level was high, so ducking the issue wouldn't be impossible. No one can tell you're level 99 just by looking at you.

"Madam, slimes are just about the only things I've ever killed. How could I be so strong? I'm just a humble witch with a simple life and no ambitions for anything more."

"Witch" is an entirely different class from "mage." Mages are the ones who fling spells around like they're going out of style, while witches are more knowledgeable about things like restorative herbs and ores. That's why I make medicines.

"Is that right? From what I heard, you have incredible stats, and you're so strong no monster or adventurer could ever defeat you."

*That's unexpectedly specific... For starters, I'll go see Natalie and find out what's actually going on.*

After finishing my meal, I visited the guild.

The woman was at the reception window, as always.

"Natalie, there's rumors going around! You told them I was level 99, didn't you? After I asked you to keep it a secret and never tell anyone, no matter what!"

"Huh…? I haven't said a word. I wouldn't do anything to betray the great Witch of the Highlands."

Natalie looked bewildered. That wasn't the expression of a liar. In that case, where did it come from?

But then something occurred to her.

"Ah, I see… Yes, that's probably it…"

"Did you remember something?"

"As I recall, when I checked your status, there was another adventurer in the guild."

"Oh…"

The guild was a public space. Yeah, even though it was a small village, it wouldn't be out of the ordinary for another adventurer or two to be there.

"That's right, yes! Mr. Ernst was there, and he's a notorious blabbermouth. I'm sure that's how word got out!"

So the one who'd overheard us was a chatty adventurer…

In that case, it was only a matter of time until the cat was completely out of the bag.

If worse came to worst, it might reach the neighboring towns and villages, too!

I held my head, but not because it hurt. During my tenure as a cog in the corporate machine, I'd had awful headaches and usually took medicine for them, but these days, I was the very picture of health.

*Think. Think. What can I do to minimize the damage?*

*That's it! I'll have her overwrite it with different information and save that.*

I checked behind me, making sure there weren't any other adventurers here now.

"Natalie, please spread a rumor that my being level 99 was an error."

"Are you telling me to lie?"

"Yes, I am. Say that I'm a perfectly normal witch who simply knows a little about botany. I'm begging you. Tell them the status slate was malfunctioning!"

*Natalie is guild personnel, which means it wouldn't be strange for her to know a lot about statuses. If she says it was a mistake, lots of people should believe her!*

"I'd feel awful saying someone with your abilities was actually weak... You're the pride of our village, great Witch..."

"Knowing about my abilities won't make anyone happy. On the contrary, jealous people could start coming out of the woodwork. At the very least, strength isn't necessary to my peaceful life. Please help me out!"

If everyone had despised me, it might have been nice to get some payback.

The villagers already had plenty of respect for me, though. I also had a good track record, the long years I'd spent helping the village through medicine and healing. Status didn't need to enter this equation.

"I understand. I mustn't cause trouble for the great Witch of the Highlands."

Natalie seemed convinced.

A little damage control seemed feasible.

First things first—I'd done what I could for now.

"Aah... You know, in terms of adventurer rank, you'd undoubtedly be an S among Ss, a legend unseen since the kingdom was founded... What a shame..."

"Maybe so, but please just deal with it."

"But it would make the name of Flatta Village famous far and wide—"

"Deal with that, too. They say fame comes at a price. There's a danger that it would bring trouble to this quiet village."

"Um, could I just tell Guild Headquarters—?"

"Absolutely not!"

I made an X sign with my arms, rejecting Natalie's request with all my might.

Up until this point, my relationship with the village had gone the way I wanted it to. I was just maintaining the status quo. Nothing wrong with that.

Afterward, I was careful never to let the villagers see my power. I hadn't shown it to them before, either, so basically all I had to do was play the part of a perfectly normal witch.

Natalie seemed to have told the people around her that the slate had been wrong, and no more villagers asked me whether I was level 99.

That put an end to the matter. I'd spend my days killing slimes and brewing potions again.

Or so I thought, until one day…

…someone knocked on the door of my house.

*Who could it be…?*

Almost no one ever knocked on my door.

For starters, the location wasn't exactly convenient.

The highland was a decent walk from the village, so getting there was a pain. It wasn't on the way to anywhere else, either, so you wouldn't just happen to be in the neighborhood to stop by.

On top of that, witches were special individuals to the villagers, so nobody just casually dropped in for a visit. People occasionally brought something to share with me, but that was about it.

Because of that, hardly anyone ever came to my house. Of course, there were emergencies—maybe a child had fallen ill and the parents wanted some medicine—and at times like that, I raced to wherever I was needed.

Since it would be terrible if someone had been taken ill, I closed the grimoire I'd been reading and headed for the entryway.

When I opened the door, I discovered a party of four adventurers.

They weren't villagers, to say the least.

For one thing, the man at the front of the group appeared to be a young swordsman. He was probably in his early twenties.

There was another swordsman with bulging muscles, a woman in a robe that clearly marked her as a mage, and a teenage cleric. Four people in all.

"Yes? What do you need?"

Had they come to inquire about any powerful monsters nearby?

I wanted to apologize to them. There was absolutely nothing except small fry.

Oh, and there were no dungeons housing fantastic treasures, either. As a matter of fact, there were no dungeons period.

All I could really offer was that the forest had plants with healing properties.

*If this has anything to do with an adventure, I'll just politely decline.*

"Are you Miss Azusa, 'the Witch of the Highlands'?" asked the young swordsman, who seemed to be the leader.

"Yes, I am. Unfortunately, this isn't a good area for adventuring. The monsters are weak, and we don't have any dungeons."

"No, it's all right. That isn't why we're here."

Then what was? Were they peddlers?

"We would like to engage you in a trial of strength."

"……Huh?"

My voice cracked. I'd never heard that proposal before.

"A trial of strength? Did you want to arm wrestle or something?"

"No. We'd like to do battle."

"I'm a witch who ekes out a living by gathering medicinal herbs. Fighting me won't make you legendary heroes."

"We heard there was a level 99 witch here."

*This rumor's everywhere!*

That adventurer in the guild really must have overheard. Even adventurers who stuck to this area traveled to the towns and villages near us, so I guess that's how it got around...

"Ha-ha-ha... That was a misunderstanding. The slate broke and gave a weird number, that's all. In terms of actual skill, I'm level 10 at most. Actually, that's probably too generous. Level 3, possibly?"

"You shouldn't lie."

The woman who looked like a magician was the one who'd spoken. She was in her late twenties.

"I'm in a similar position, so I can tell. The mana is practically rolling off you. There's no mistake. You're phenomenal."

*Argh! You can tell from things like that?!*

*What is this? Are we like Stand users who are drawn to one another?*

*Still, I'm not fighting, no matter what. I mean it. If I get into one battle, I'll never be able to stop.*

"So—I'm just speaking hypothetically, all right? But even assuming I were a witch with genuine skills, I'd still have no reason to fight you."

*That's a perfectly sound argument. I'll stick with that one.*

I don't run a dojo here, so there's no point in anyone trying to beat me.

"You see, we want to get stronger. Please spar with us and help us!"

*They're polite, but I really don't want to involve myself with this.*

This was a problem. If I didn't get these people to go home, my peace and quiet would be ruined.

*If it's come to this, maybe I can fool them with a lie.*

I cleared my throat and began.


"The truth is, long ago, I once grew drunk on my own power."
*Never happened.


"We didn't know…"

They were listening more earnestly than I expected. I felt a bit guilty.


"I hurt many people. Some even lost their lives to my attack spells."
*The only thing I've killed is slimes.


"And so, I resolved never to fight again."
*Everything about this is true.

"So even great adventurers have painful pasts..."

"Yes, and as a result, I can't fight with you. Please understand."
*Seriously, I'm begging you. Take a hint.

*They'll probably give up now.*
"We understand how you feel, Miss Azusa. We'll withdraw."
"Thank you very much. May the road you travel be a bright one."
"Many more adventurers like us are bound to come to you, and it's probably going to be a lot of trouble. Be careful not to let anyone ambush you. Some adventurers only care about making a name for themselves."
*Hold it.*
"Have the stories about me spread that far?"
*Now there's a nasty piece of news.*
"Yes. I doubt there's an adventurer in this territory who hasn't heard about you by now. Besides, the local adventurers are very proud that Azusa, their 'Witch of the Highlands,' is the strongest being around."
*What do they think they're doing, making me the pride of the region?! I wish they'd quit sabotaging my R & R.*
*No help for it. I'll change my strategy.*
"All right. I will spar with you, and only you, just this once."
"Do you mean it?!"
A wave of enthusiasm surged through the party. They were treating me like some sort of celebrity.
"On one condition, though: If you lose, I want you to go around telling people the Witch of the Highlands was nothing special. If possible, I want to avoid fighting."
The female magician nodded vigorously.
"All right. Sparring or no, I'd hate to seriously injure you, so..."
I went outside and used a farming hoe to draw a big circle in the dirt. It was more of an oval than a perfect circle, but it would serve.

"Let's say whoever steps outside this circle loses. Is that all right with you?"

Of course, no one declined, and the matter was settled.

This way, we'd be able to finish up fast without anyone getting hurt.

"If I leave the circle, I lose. If every one of you leaves the circle, your side loses. Let's do it that way. Oh, and anyone who steps outside is out of the match at that point."

Those conditions favored my opponents, so I doubted they'd complain.

"Well then, let's get right to it!"

As if to declare that victory went to the swift, the magician girl thrust her staff out in front of her and chanted something.

"O wind, choose this moment to become my servant and raise a tempest..."

Naturally, she'd thought of using the wind to hurl me out. That had been my plan, too.

*Fooooooooom!*

A cyclone twisted my way. Just from the noise, I could tell it would pack a punch. Apparently, these adventurers were fairly high-level.

*Is that how you use Whirlwind magic?*

That had been one of the skills in my status, but I hadn't really known how to use it. Granted, I'd activated the Ice and Snow spell with a random chant, so maybe there wasn't any strict protocol.

It wasn't that I had no steps to take.

*I dub this "Operation Eye for an Eye."*

"O wind, choose this moment to become my servant and raise a tempest!"

I chanted the exact same words as my opponent. To put it bluntly, I stole 'em. No such thing as copyright in *this* world!

*FOOOOOOOOOOOOOOOOOOOOOOOM!*

A whirlwind several dozen times larger than my opponent's formed...

...and headed straight for the other group!

First, it swallowed the magician girl's whirlwind and absorbed it. That didn't negate my vortex; on the contrary, it sped up.

"I've never seen a whirlwind like that!" "It's a monster!" "Run!"

My opponents were all taken aback. The storm was just that enormous.

It was safe to say that the moment I'd used magic, they'd lost their will to fight.

If the whirlwind pulled them in, I'd probably be able to send them out of the circle at the very least.

All of my opponents took a direct hit from my tempest. *Great, it worked!*

*Except I think it might have been a bit too strong.*

"Eeeeeeeeeeeeek!"

"Aaaaaaaaaaaugh!"

"Help meeeeeee!"

Now trapped in the funnel, the party was being blown farther and farther away.

Shoot! I'd underestimated the power of level 99!

This went way beyond "outside the circle"!

The whirlwind gradually weakened with time, however, and at last, the adventurers seemed to touch down softly.

…Right next to the village of Flatta, at the base of the hill.

"Oh, crap…"

Frankly, they'd landed in the worst possible location.


After that, just to make sure, I went to the village.

"To think you'd send a veteran party flying with a single whirlwind! That's our great Witch of the Highlands!"

"I saw your true power clearly with my own eyes, great Witch!"

"Now our village's future is secure for several hundred years! You really are level 99, aren't you?!"

The fact that I'd trounced that party was already the talk of the village.

Well, of course it was. This place was at the foot of the highlands, and they had to have seen that enormous spell…

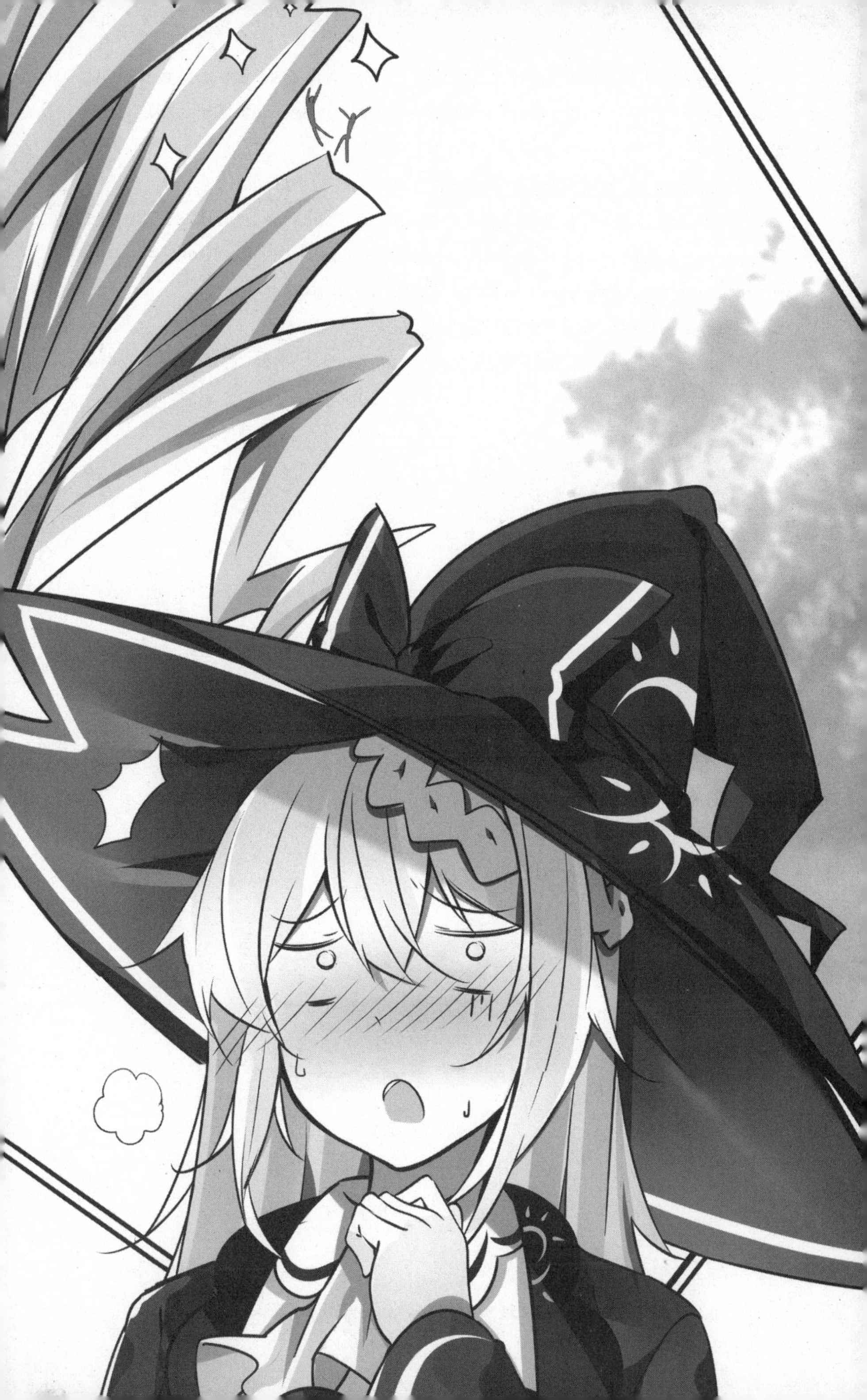

"Everyone in that party said they were going to start again from square one! They said that, someday, they'd be just like you, great Witch!"

*Hey, they were talking about me! That wasn't the deal!*

That said, since I'd launched them into the sky in front of witnesses, there was probably no way to hide it. Lying and telling them a brutal monster had appeared would send the village into a panic...

"Yes. I blew them away with magic."

That the Witch of the Highlands was level 99 was now official, and everyone knew it.

After my true skills became public knowledge (against my will), I sent away for books on monsters and began studying.

I hadn't developed the urge to slay monsters. Quite the opposite, in fact.

I did it because if I knew enough about monsters, I could give advice to anyone who came asking me to slay one, which meant I could get by without going anywhere.

I wouldn't mind offering them some help. I just didn't want anyone working me like a dog.

After all, I'm level 99. Even I know that that's vanishingly rare in this world.

If all the troublemakers banded together and showed up at my house, it would be an utter disaster.

It had been only ten days since I'd flung that party off my hill, so my life hadn't changed much. No one had asked me to kill a dragon or anything yet.

The sole difference was that the medicines I sold on consignment through the general store were going faster, so I'd begun gathering more herbs.

People probably believed that remedies made by a level-99 witch would be extra effective. Frankly, there's not much difference.

"This isn't a wired society; maybe information takes a while to travel. It sure would be great if the news died down without spreading."

Saying that aloud might have been a bad idea, because somebody started banging loudly on my door.

Who was it this time?

It was unlikely that such rough blows were coming from a villager.

If I pretended I wasn't home, they were liable to break the door down, so I hastily opened it.

If they wanted me to help them slay a dragon, I'd teach them a good method for vanquishing the beast and send the visitor on their way. I hoped there were no emergencies or villages in danger of being destroyed.

"Yes, who is it?"

Something enormous stood in front of me.

It was tall. Not only that, it wasn't human.

*Big wings. A big body. Can probably breathe fire. Has a pair of horns.*

A dragon had dropped by.

In fact, it had been using its tail to knock. Hence the violent thuds.

"Um…may I ask what brings you here?"

According to the books I'd read, dragons were higher monsters, so they understood human speech.

That it had even knocked on the door at all implied such intelligence.

My book learning was coming in handy right off the bat, but I really wished this hadn't been the scenario in which it was paying off…

"Here in the province of Nanterre, dragons are said to be the strongest monsters, and I, Laika, am renowned as the strongest of all dragons."

*So dragons don't just understand human speech—they can use it?*

Its voice was so loud that it reverberated in my head. It felt like being at a concert.

"And what might a dragon such as yourself need with me?"

"Recently, I've been hearing rumors that the strongest witch in existence lives here."

"Don't tell me you've come to test your strength…?"

"You're sharp. That saves time."

*Just how far has that rumor traveled?*

*I'd at least like to keep it limited to the human race.*

This could not have been worse… No one had asked me to go defeat a dragon. The dragon had come to me!

"I don't want to be known as the 'strongest' anything. I just accumulated experience points little by little over three centuries until it became a huge number, that's all. I'll concede the title of strongest to you."

"As if I could settle for that! Fight me. Let's make this clear, once and for all!"

*What a thundering nuisance.*

*As I keep saying, I don't run a dojo, so don't come by to bust it.*

"What would you do if I said I don't want to?"

"First I'd trample your house flat. Then I'd lay waste to your garden."

*Looks like I've got no choice but to fight…*

If I lost my house, I'd never be able to relax and take life easy.

"All right. Let's do it. However, I'm not claiming to be the strongest, so if I turn out to be much weaker than you, go easy on me, if you would."

"Very well. As long as I'm able to confirm I am indeed superior, that will be enough for me."

We found an area with lots of wide-open space, away from the house. After all, I couldn't have my home getting wrecked in the course of the battle.

"Now then, I'll show you the true power of Laika!"

"Yes, yes, by all means, be my guest."

The dragon flapped its wings and soared into the air.

"I'll burn you to ash!"

It spit flames from its mouth!

No way was I going to take the brunt of that. No serious burns for me, thank you.

"Freeze everything!"

I slammed an Ice and Snow spell into the flames.

My maneuver seemed to have worked. The spells collided, canceling and erasing the flames.

"*Tch!* Not bad! So you really are a high-level witch, then!"

*Guess I can't pretend to lose on purpose, either.*

*In the end, using my true power and defeating it quickly might be the most efficient method.*

*Well, what's the best tactic here? After all, my opponent is airborne.*

"I now briefly bid the ground farewell!"

I chanted, casting a Levitation spell.

Now you could say I was technically even with the dragon.

I use Levitation often because it makes getting home from Flatta easier.

*So, how should I fight from here on out?*

*I don't really want to get too close. That means I'll be using magic, but I doubt a whirlwind could blow away an opponent of this size as easily as a human. Even if I did manage to knock my visitor out of the sky, if it fell on the village, it would cause massive damage.*

A Lightning Attack, then? To be honest, though, I didn't think I could control my power. Unlike slimes, dragons were highly intelligent, and if I killed one, I suspected I'd feel guilty. I'd do my best not to take its life.

That left Flame or Ice and Snow.

Dragons actually breathed fire, so flames might not do anything to them.

So it would have to be Ice and Snow.

"Mimic me and fly, will you? The insolence!"

The dragon raised a hand to slap me out of the air, but I evaded easily.

That empty swing left the dragon vulnerable.

I slipped right in close to it.

"I'll burn you out of the sky!" The dragon opened its mouth, preparing to spit fire again.

Just what I'd been waiting for.

I sent an Ice and Snow spell right at its mouth.

"Freeze everything!"

The dragon's jaw was immobilized in a burst of frost.

In one stroke, its mouth had been turned into an ice cave.

"Agwuh! Ugh! Bluguuuuuuuuh!"

The dragon panicked, then dropped down to the ground and started running around.

I'd done it. This way, I'd plunged my opponent into confusion without having to take its life.

"Well? Got brain freeze?"

The dragon was so flustered it was pitiful. You could tell just by watching it run helter-skelter.

*Wait. Running around?*

I had a bad feeling about this...

"Don't you wreck my house! Whatever you do, don't wreck it!"

"Ugwuuuuuuuh! Coooooooooooold!"

But the dragon ran toward the house—and it bumped into a corner. *Crunch.*

The room on that corner caved in.

My anger flared.

"Look, I told you not to wreck it!"

I got in close to the dragon—

"This is the pain of my demolished room!"

—and I punched it!

"Bwaaaah...!"

That one hit knocked the dragon out, and it toppled right over onto the plain.

It didn't seem to be dead, but the damage was great enough that it wouldn't be able to move for a little while.

Since I had punched it, to no one's surprise, my hand hurt. I should just consider myself lucky it wasn't broken.

"Wh-what power... To think I'd fall so ingloriously..."

The dragon seemed unable to believe the circumstances in which it found itself.

"For starters, that's a win for me, but more importantly..."

I looked at my damaged house. I was absolutely going to make sure I was fairly compensated.

"Listen, Laika the dragon."

I went up to the beast and poked it.

"You'd better fix my house. If you don't, I'll never forgive you."

My face was smiling, but I don't think my eyes were.

Apparently, they managed to convince the dragon that I was more than willing to fight.

"A-all right... I'll do something about it, s-so...spare me... Don't take my life..."

"I wouldn't do that. If I did, I couldn't make you fix this for me, could I? It isn't insured, you know."

It didn't look as if the bedroom had been damaged, but there could have been a draft... *Maybe I'd better stay at the village inn for a while.*

"Um...I have a fair amount of money saved up at the mountain where I make my home. Would it be all right if I returned to get it? I'd like to use it to cover the repairs..."

Come to think of it, I'd heard that dragons tended to collect gold.

"That's fine, but know that if you run, I'll come put you down."

"I swear to keep my promise!"

The dragon flew off, somewhat unsteadily.

That day, I went to the village to find lodgings.

"Oh! Great Witch! You must have defeated the dragon!"

"We saw the wyrm very clearly, even from the village!"

"To think you'd defeat that creature! I'd expect no less, great Witch!"

*So they all knew. Figures.*

Dragons were huge, and even from a distance, they were hard not to notice.

"I'm sorry. I did beat the dragon, but part of my house caved in, so I've come to stay at the village inn for a short while. I'm sorry to have disturbed you."

"No, no! The dragon's to blame!"

"Actually, you protected this village from that dragon!"

"I'll show you to the best room at the inn!"

"You fool! No inn in the village is suitable lodgings for the great Witch!"

The conversation went back and forth a few times, and in the end, I wound up staying in the guest room at the village hall. That was where royal officials stayed when they came here on business.

Maybe it wasn't a bad idea to take people up on their kindness once in a while.

Donating some expensive medicines later would probably balance the books.

Since I was staying the night, I took a leisurely walk through the village for the first time in a long while. The place seemed livelier than it had when I'd first arrived three hundred years ago. More people, too.

There were probably several reasons for that, but from what I heard, I was one of them. The villagers often told me so.

It was because I'd made such valuable medicines for the village.

In every village, people died of illnesses or injuries before reaching the end of their natural lives. Because of the potions I provided, the risk of death was substantially lower here than in the surrounding villages.

In particular, the significant decrease in deaths from childhood sickness was contributing to the rising population. I also made something like nutrition supplements for children, in addition to remedies for when they were ill.

As far as I was concerned, gathering herbs and making medicines was akin to a hobby, part of my laid-back routine. If I was managing to save lives through that hobby, I was terribly honored.

Since I didn't need to go back home that day, I decided to take it easy at the tavern and enjoy a drink at my leisure.

Even at night, the tavern was hopping.

"Hey, it's the great Witch!"

"A toast to the great Witch!"

Many of the customers were already three sheets to the wind, and the place was a free-for-all.

I was shown to a table.

For some reason, they brought me an expensive-looking drink I hadn't asked for.

"Um, I haven't placed an order yet..."

"When I was a child, your medicine saved me, great Witch." The owner's daughter smiled as she spoke. "This is a thank-you. Please take your time and enjoy your drink."

It had been like this all day. Nobody was letting me pay for anything.

I guess a day like that isn't so bad every once in a while.

I sipped my liquor slowly, savoring it.

My tenure as an office worker had been busy. To be frank, I was little more than a slave to the company.

I'd almost never had the sense that my work was helping anyone. Honestly, I'd have to say my efforts were solely for the sake of the company. So it follows that, no matter how busy I was, my entire time there had been meaningless.

Interacting with people doesn't go against my "laid-back life" creed in and of itself. Maybe I should visit the village a little more often.

The expensive liquor tasted quite different from what I usually drank. It was so mellow. I bet that's what made it expensive.

"Aaaaah, that's delicious. Compared with long ago, this is heaven."

*Didn't mean to say that out loud.*

"With you protecting our lives, great Witch, we're living in heaven, too!"

"When I was young, I spent a long time traveling, and there's no better village than Flatta!"

They were praising me to my face, so I took it with several grains of salt, but still, it made me happy.

"I'm glad I ended up living near this village as well," I said, and I meant it.

*I'm proud of this place. I'd like to keep watching it grow.*

That day, I got pleasantly drunk, then went back to my lodgings and slept.

I was a little late getting to bed, but it was still earlier than when I got to knock off during my stint as a corporate slave. Besides, back then, I'd had to wake up around six in the morning... Even though it was three centuries ago, I remembered it vividly.

The breakfast they gave me was rather extravagant for the village as well. They were treating me like an official honored guest.

"I'm glad I'm a witch..."

I ate breakfast. The milk in particular was incredibly good, maybe because it was fresh from the cow.

The food here was seasoned more simply than in Japan, and it always seemed to end up tasting flat. When it came to milk, though, the village of Flatta won, hands down. Packaged milk couldn't begin to compare. A hearty thanks to the cows and everyone who made the food!

I know—maybe I'll teach them a bit about cooking one of these days. I still remember how from my years in Japan, so I should be able to improvise some recipes to teach them.

As I absently mulled over this, the person in charge of the cooking strode quickly up to me.

"Great Witch of the Highlands, there's someone here to see you."

"Have them wait in a free meeting room, then. I'll be done with my meal in three minutes."

Wondering which villager it would be this time, I stepped into the meeting room.

The young girl waiting for me had a pair of horns protruding from her head.

She looked about the right age for middle school—thirteen or so.

Her clothes had a bit of Lolita flair to them, and the outfit suited her so well that it was obviously her everyday getup, not cosplay.

Who was she?

I'd never seen a horned villager before.

Actually, the horns meant she wasn't a normal human, didn't they?

"I fear I caused you a lot of trouble yesterday."

When our eyes met, the girl bowed politely.

"Um…yesterday? I don't believe we've met…"

There was no way I'd forget someone with horns.

"Oh, I've transformed, so it's possible you don't recognize me."

Transformed? I didn't rescue a crane or a Jizou statue.

"I'm Laika, the dragon from yesterday."

"Say what?! Wait, you're a girl?!"

Come to think of it, Laika is a rather feminine name…

"Many members of the dragon race have abundant mana, and we are able to adopt human shapes. If we enter a human village without doing so, we end up causing a panic," said Laika the dragon girl.

True, if a dragon showed up at a village, it would probably throw the place into a terrible uproar. Even if the villagers mobilized everyone in town, a battle would be hopeless against such an enormous creature.

"You aren't a 'girl' age-wise, though, are you?"

She couldn't actually be thirteen, not when presenting herself in such a dignified manner.

"I believe it's been about three hundred years since I was born."

"So we're around the same age, then."

It seemed odd to talk about being "around the same age" when you were three hundred, but it was what it was, so I just had to roll with it.

"Also…please accept this."

Laika set a large cloth sack on the table.

It seemed too heavy for a young girl to lift, but her true nature as a dragon meant it probably wasn't an issue.

"What's this?"

I peeked inside, and the answer immediately presented itself.

Gold coins.

"This is the money for the repairs, then."

"Yes, that's right. I brought all the money I've saved."

*You're thriftier than I expected, dragon.*

"Thank you. With this much, repairs shouldn't be a problem."

If all we were doing was restoring my house, this seemed likely to cover it, so I was relieved.

However, Laika was fidgeting as if she still had something to say.

*Don't tell me there's a girl with an intractable illness who needs this money to live? Does she have a reason like that?*

I'm not an ogre. If there are extenuating circumstances, I'll take them into account.

"Um, actually, I had a request..."

"What is it? It won't cost you anything; say as much as you like."

"Could you possibly take me as...y-your apprentice?"

I stared blankly at her.

"Apprentice? I'd be your teacher, you mean?"

"Yes. Fighting you made me painfully aware I am still inexperienced, great Witch. I wish to discard my vain pride in being the strongest in the province of Nanterre and start my studies over from the beginning."

"That's a lovely resolution, but...a-an apprentice?"

*I've lived three hundred years, and I've never once entertained that idea.*

"Um, listen, I think it would be a bad idea for me to hide it, so I'm going to tell you. I didn't acquire my power through any sort of special training. I just routinely killed slimes around the neighborhood for a very long time, the experience points piled up, and here I am."

So I really had nothing to teach her.

"No, that buildup of my efforts is exactly what I would like to study! I was overconfident in my power as a dragon, grew arrogant, and I neglected to hone my skills. The result was ignominious defeat!"

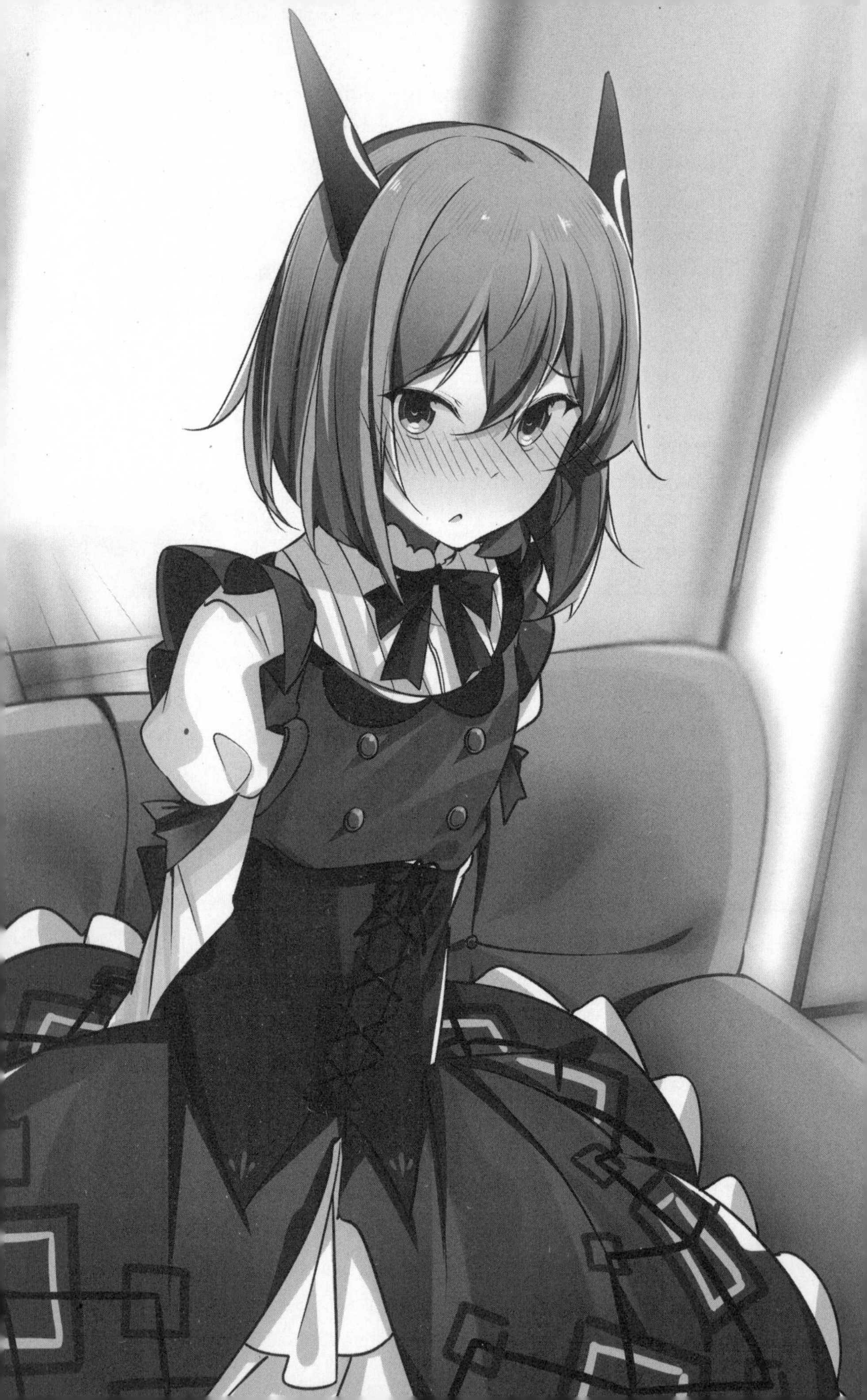

*This dragon-girl is more earnest than I thought.*

"But in that case, what should I teach you?"

If I wasn't going to pass on any new skills to her, there was no point in taking her on as an apprentice, was there?

"I would appreciate the opportunity to live with you, earn my keep, and study your lifestyle."

*A roommate, hmm?* To be honest, I really wasn't keen on that idea. Unlike lazing around by yourself, living with another person generates stress.

Besides, I'd lived alone for three hundred years, so it seemed a bit late to start sharing my space...

*Hang on.*

"You said 'earn your keep'?"

"Yes."

"Meaning you'll cook and clean and things? I mean, I wouldn't make you do absolutely everything, but..."

"Of course I will. Asking you to handle the cooking and cleaning on top of making me your apprentice would be far too much."

My resolve had begun weakening a bit.

*In that case, it might be okay...*

It was also true that, having lived alone for three centuries, I'd fallen into a bit of a rut.

At this point, you could practically call it tradition. No one in Japan had ever lived alone for such an extended period of time. I had my own established views on single occupancy.

*But it might be all right to close the book on that tradition...*

"All right. I'll let you become my apprentice."

"Thank you very much!"

Laika bowed her head courteously, pointing her two adorable horns at me.

After three hundred years of witchhood, I'd acquired an apprentice.

However, if we were actually going to be living together, we would need to make a few improvements.

"Listen, Laika, just repairing my house isn't enough now. Honestly, we need to think about expanding it."

"What do you mean, great Witch?"

I'd ask her to call me something besides "great Witch" later, but for now, I decided to settle the issue at hand.

"You'll be living here, too, you know. If all we do are repairs, it'll be too cramped. We'll have to add another room."

"I see. Yes, you're right."

Originally, a married couple had lived here, but it had worked for them because they were, in fact, married. There was a greater sense of distance between teachers and apprentices, and having a little more space would make things easier on both of us.

For an apprentice, constantly being in close proximity to someone who outranks you would probably be rough psychologically.

If it had been me living in the same house as my boss, I would have developed new ulcers every single day.

"And so, until the upgraded house is finished, I'll be staying in the village. You should stay at the inn as well."

"In that case, shall I take this opportunity to build it for you?"

I hadn't expected that response. *What, is she a carpenter?*

"'Build it'? You aren't a licensed architect, are you?"

"As long as I have wood and stone to use, the rest is just assembly work, and that's simple. Leave it to me, please."

Laika thumped her chest to show she could do it.

Since she was just a dragon masquerading as a human, she sure didn't seem qualified to build a house. Still, if she was going to insist that strongly, maybe I would leave it to her.

"I have the right to use the area of the forest where I gather medicinal herbs, so go ahead and take trees from there. I'll let you handle the layout and design."

"Thank you very much! I'll create something to your liking, great Witch!"

"Oh, I'll go with you, just in case."

After all, I had no clue whether I could trust a dragon's aesthetics wholesale.

Once outside the village, Laika reverted to her dragon form.

"It will be easier if we fly, so I'll travel in this shape. It's also easier for me to exercise my strength this way."

*She really is the dragon I fought.*

*We may be outside the village, but they'll be able to see us from there for sure. I'll have to explain this to them later.*

"Climb onto my back, great Witch. I'll go straight to the forest."

"Do you think you could stop calling me 'great Witch'?"

Laika's apprenticeship to a witch meant she was a sort of witch-in-training as well. We were practitioners of the same craft. If I was going to be addressed constantly, something else would feel more appropriate.

"We're going to be living together, so just call me by my name—Azusa."

"In that case, I shall call you Lady Azusa."

*I suppose tacking* lady *on is all right. I am going to be her teacher anyway.*

I climbed onto Laika's back.

It wasn't uncomfortable up there. At the very least, I didn't feel I was at risk of falling.

"I'll be flying, so tell me which direction the forest is in, if you would."

*This is kinda like a taxi*, I thought.

◇

Laika traveled quite fast in dragon form, and we reached the forest before long.

It took time on foot only because of the elevation, and as the crow flew, it wasn't very far. There are things you notice from the air, too.

Once we were in the forest, she snapped trees one after another. Apparently, a dragon's strength is enough to break large trunks like it's nothing.

But my attack power beat this dragon, so what's up with that?

"Just so you know, don't line up broken trees and tell me it's a house. Make it so drafts won't get in."

"I know. I'm only doing it this way because I don't have a saw to make lumber. I'll turn them into proper boards later."

She was telling the truth.

Laika flew to a town somewhere, returning a little while later with all sorts of tools.

"While I was in town, I looked at several buildings and studied how they were made. I believe I'll be able to build a good house."

"Can you learn construction just by looking?"

"Dragons generally have good memories."

Laika immediately started processing the trees she'd gathered.

She said that, as a dragon, she'd be too big and her hands would fumble things, so she did this part in human form.

Frankly, she was insanely fast. By the time the sun went down, she'd already started on the construction.

One of the reasons was that her dragon strength allowed her to carry the materials without much effort.

True, if you were building a house in Japan, things would definitely go faster if a wooden pillar weighed only a few hundred grams.

When you were the size of a dragon, designing a building to house humans was a bit like an advanced game of building blocks. She was using a construction method based on slotting components together and avoiding nails as much as possible.

It was the technique of Japan's shrine and temple carpenters. No doubt it was fair game for buildings that weren't shrines or temples, as well, so it wasn't too strange for a being who lived in a different culture to employ it.

That said, fast as she was, there was no way she'd finish on the very first day, and the sky was getting dark.

"Why don't we call it a day? Let's go back to the village. I'll find you a place to stay, too."

I clapped my hands, signaling we were done. Either way, I needed to let the village know I'd taken a dragon as an apprentice.

"No, Lady Azusa. I'm not tired, so I can keep going."

Something about those words rubbed me the wrong way.

"Dragons have excellent night vision. If I work all night, I'll finish tomorrow."

*Oh, this isn't good.*

"Nope, no way, none of that!!!" I barked.

Laika flinched, and her hands paused in the middle of their task.

"Um, have I committed an error of some sort, Lady Azusa...?"

"Laika, you told me you could pull an all-nighter, didn't you? You can't do that. Really and truly, you can't!"

"I, um... I thought I'd get it done, no matter what..."

"It's not okay to say 'no matter what' too often as if it's a good thing!"

I was remembering my days as a corporate slave.

*If I make myself do overtime today, things will work out somehow.*

*If I pull an all-nighter, I can catch up.*

Over and over, I'd pushed myself with those beliefs.

And what was the result? I'd ended up with a schedule where pushing myself was the norm.

You've already seen the consequences.

Eventually, I'd pushed myself to my death. In short, that's what comes of getting it done "no matter what."

I was through with "no matter what."

We'd worked all the way to sunset. The rest would keep until tomorrow.

"Look, it's dark, isn't it? That's proof that the world is telling us it's time to stop for the day. At the very least, I didn't get stronger by pushing myself. All I did was make a habit of living moderately."

"I understand. I'll do as you say, Lady Azusa."

"Good, that's right."

I smiled.

I had to be able to manage my subordinate's labor properly.

"From now on, whenever you get tired or feel like you can't do something anymore, don't hesitate to speak up."

"My heart aches at your consideration for your apprentice, Lady Azusa..."

*That's a little much, don't you think?*

I intentionally had her go back to the village in dragon form, then switch to being human just outside. If I'd made her charge in as a dragon, she might have bumped into a building.

People had gathered to see what the heck was going on, so in a way, it was perfect.

"Friends, as of today, the dragon Laika has become my apprentice. She may unintentionally cause trouble for you, but she's a good, considerate girl. Please treat her with affection."

As I spoke to them, Laika bowed.

"If Laika commits any transgressions, contact me, her teacher. I'll scold her properly."

*The villagers still look uneasy... Well, they do have a dragon right in front of them, so there's probably no getting around that.*

Naban the cheesemaker raised a hand.

"Erm, great Witch... Dragons are strong, aren't they? Is it possible she might drink and suddenly fly into a rage...?"

"The same is true for me and every other powerful adventurer. Of course, as her teacher, I'll check to make sure my apprentice doesn't get drunk and cause a scene."

*I know what this reminds me of. It's like taking a new subordinate on a visit to a client company. You have to understand the client's perspective, but at the same time, you have to protect your colleague.*

Finally, the village chief came over to me.

I repeated what I'd said a minute ago.

"All right, Laika. Tell them in your own words."

She looked a bit tense but gave a small nod. I had her personally tell the villagers why she wanted to study under me.

"I am the dragon Laika, and I've just apprenticed myself to Lady Azusa, 'the Witch of the Highlands'! I look forward to making your acquaintance! Naturally, when I am in the village, I will use this girl form, not my dragon form!"

Witnessing her commendable attitude, the village chief's expression softened.

"All right. I will permit the dragon Laika to come and live in the village. Having a dragon around will serve to deter evildoers from outside as well."

We'd gotten permission from the village chief.

"That's right. If the great Witch is keeping an eye on her, I doubt there'll be any problems."

"She looks a lot more intelligent than my girl."

"It would be ungrateful of us to reject the great Witch's apprentice anyway."

The villagers had also accepted the situation.

Thus, Laika was granted citizenship.

That day, it was decided Laika would spend the night in the guest room with me.

We had some time before dinner, so we relaxed in the room.

As proof that I trusted her, I told her my current status. Laika seemed more surprised by the number of spells than by any of the numeric values.

"I knew it. All those spells mean you really are a legendary witch, Lady Azusa."

"Do you think so?"

For dinner, we went to my favorite restaurant, the Savvy Eagle. Laika ate with me, of course.

"Lady Azusa, thank you for what you said earlier."

"What? Oh, for talking to the villagers, you mean?"

"As I am a dragon, I have always made others obey me by demonstrating my power, no matter the situation. However, being accepted through a method other than strength was a valuable experience for me. I was genuinely happy."

*I see. This is more than just training a new worker. I'll have to get a dragon used to life as a human as well.*

"That's a good direction to move in. Keep it up."

"Of course! Thank you in advance for your help!"

Laika was pretty accustomed to using a knife and fork.

She must have been mingling with people in towns for a very long time.

"Have you spent a lot of time living as a human?"

"Yes, though I never actually lived in a town. Only a very few people are able to tell when a dragon is in human shape, so I've hardly ever had any trouble."

Fantasy worlds had beast-men as well, and maybe a feature as minor as horns could be explained away. No beast-men lived in Flatta, but traveling beast-men sometimes came through.

"Well, the village has accepted you now. Let's work to build a good house tomorrow, too."

"Yes! I'll do an excellent job!"

◇

The next morning, Laika got right down to work on the addition again.

I went along as her supervisor.

"Things are progressing smoothly at the moment, and I have not had any real problems."

"It sure seems that way from where I stand."

She was so fast it was hard to believe houses could be built so quickly. This was also thanks to her dragon strength.

"By the way, Laika, how high are your stats?"

Since I'd won, mine were probably higher, but I wondered how great the difference was.

I was just curious.

"I've never had it measured, so I'm not certain, but I've been known as the strongest dragon in Nanterre for roughly a hundred years."

That's a long time to be at the top.

As an aside, the province of Nanterre includes these highlands and the surrounding area, and it feels a bit like Switzerland. Mountains are abundant here, so I'm not surprised dragons would choose to live in Nanterre.

*I've never been to Switzerland, so I'm saying this only because it feels like the thing to say right about now.

"I wonder if we shouldn't get you registered with the guild as an adventurer. I'll leave the decision to you. I'm not planning to put you through special training based on your numbers or anything."

"True, it could serve as an index, but unless I acquire strength that satisfies me, it's meaningless."

From the sound of it, Laika wasn't that interested in things like status.

It was probably because she was a dragon. Meeting a dragon would be enough to make most people grovel.

Conversely, if you're human, it's hard to tell what sort of power you have unless you show your status.

Because of that, I think we tend to use status to make others view our own strength objectively.

By the time noon drew near, it was possible to make out what sort of structure this was shaping up to be.

The original house had acquired a log cabin addition.

It reminded me of the summer residences you might see at Karuizawa, and it fit right in up in the highlands.

"Brick houses or buildings with stained-glass windows would have required specialized artisans, so I decided to use wood."

"Yes, this is fine. Keep doing what you're doing. I think we should break for lunch soon, though. Let's go to the village to eat."

"No, I'll reach a better stopping point very soon, so I'll keep going..."

"Laika. Did you forget what I said yesterday?"

*When it's time to rest, you rest. Don't make a virtue of working too much. As long as I'm around, I won't tolerate poor working conditions.*

"No, it isn't that I want to work a lot... It's only that stopping when things feel this half-finished will bother me."

"In that case, reach a good stopping point within the next ten minutes."

"Yes, ma'am!"

Work-life balance, work-life balance. I feel like a human resources manager.

In the village, we ate something pasta-like for lunch, and I had Laika drink a lot of water.

She'd been doing physical labor for a significant length of time, so I wanted her to rehydrate.

Parenthetically, the village of Flatta has abundant groundwater, so that resource is in no short supply.

After our meal, Laika and I took a leisurely walk through the village.

There was a reason for that, too: I wanted to get the villagers used to seeing her face sooner rather than later.

I thought I'd have her register at the guild while we were at it, but as that felt like it would count as work hours in a way, I left it for another day.

If I only wanted to exchange magic stones, I could do that on my own.

Then the afternoon construction work began.

We'd made considerable progress, and it felt as if we'd entered the final stretch.

The walls were done, so she began putting the wooden roof on.

Finally, we carried chairs and tables made from the extra lumber into the building.

I'd helped with that bit. The wood really was surprisingly easy to cut, and I hadn't gotten tired. Clearly, my level was indeed high.

By evening, the remodel of the house in the highlands had been completed without any mishaps.

"Yes, splendid!"

Looking at it from outside, I felt satisfied.

The room that had been partially demolished earlier had been turned into an enclosed corridor that led to the addition, a log cabin–style area with a peaked roof.

The cabin had its own external door, so it was possible to enter directly.

The addition had a high ceiling and rooms on its second story.

On the first floor, in addition to a shared space, there were three individual rooms. Meaning, my apprentice's privacy was guaranteed.

Even if I picked up more apprentices, we'd be able to accommodate them.

I mean, at this point, I had absolutely no intention of doing that, but...

"Excellent work, Laika."

"I'm very glad it pleases you, Lady Azusa."

Laika seemed rather pleased herself.

Since she appeared to be the same age as a middle-school girl, the expression was very cute on her.

"All right. We'll need to go back to the village and tell them the house is finished. They may be getting the guest room ready for us again today."

"Thank you very much for doing so much to help me fit in in the village."

There she went again. Laika was probably raised very well.

"I said I'd be your teacher. I'm only doing what a teacher would do. I haven't done anything special."

It was nothing to brag about. It was only natural to take care of my apprentice.

People didn't have to avoid her simply because she was a dragon. After all, no matter how you looked at her, she was a person.

"Well, let's have ourselves a feast in the village today, shall we? Wait, can dragons eat human food?"

Up until now, she'd eaten the same food as I had as if it was normal, but...

"Yes. When I'm transformed as a human, I'm able to eat like one."

Apparently, it was no cause for concern.

"If I eat enough to fill a human's belly, it provides enough nutrition for me to survive as a dragon."

That ability seemed a bit like cheating...

If we always flew, I wouldn't get enough exercise, so we walked to the village.

On the way, we ran into slimes again, so we took them out.

Laika swiped at one with a hand like she was fanning dust away and sent it flying.

That was all it took to finish it off. It was an attack from a dragon, after all.

"Come to think of it, I've never killed slimes before. There were none on the mountain where I lived."

"They're a low-level monster, besides."

"Somehow, fighting them at all seems like a waste of time. I mean, it doesn't even feel like a battle."

"You'd think so, wouldn't you? It's important to do this and stick with it, though. As the proverb says, 'Slow and steady wins the race.'"

I went out of my way to sound teacherly.

As a matter of fact, since I couldn't teach her any techniques, it was really the only thing I could say.

"Certainly, if we dragons had been killing slimes for ages, we might have become even stronger by now. I will emulate your way of life, teacher."

"That's right. I think patience is probably key."

Maybe because we were deliberately confronting slimes, it took us about five minutes longer than usual to reach the village.

However, at the village entrance, Laika began peering intently at the air, then gazing at the ground.

Her eyes darted around as if this were her first visit.

"Is something bothering you?"

"To be honest, yes," Laika admitted.

"I'm the type who worries about these things forever, so don't hint. Just tell me."

"This village's magical defenses are extremely weak. If a single evil magician came here, it could turn into a sea of flames in an instant."

"Ah, well, there's no point in assuming worst-case scenarios like that."

"But that isn't all. No measures have been taken against land-based attacks, either. If a large monster went on a rampage, it would get into the village right away. Even in a fight with humans, it'd be conquered immediately."

It might have been because she was a dragon, but Laika seemed to focus rather heavily on combat when she looked at things.

"Of course, I do think that's because this village has always been peaceful. However, there's no guarantee it will remain so forever."

"Y-you might be overthinking…"

I'd lived three hundred years so far, and since this village didn't have much strategic value, even during a war, I didn't think anyone would see it as a problem.

"The information that you are the strongest has begun spreading only recently, though, Lady Azusa. It isn't a given that some coward won't take the village hostage in an attempt to defeat you."

At that point, Laika cleared her throat, flushing a bit.

"Of course, I fought you fairly, without doing anything so spineless," she added, pointing out she wasn't that type.

"Yes. You were quite honorable there."

"Even so, we don't know whether things will change in the future. Word of the great witch reached my mountain, and that's more than two full days from this village as the human walks."

"You have a point."

I had to make sure the village didn't suffer because of me, no matter what.

I couldn't allow that.

"Should we relocate to the village, then? But we just rebuilt the house, and I'd hate to move right away…"

*And anyway, I'm not SEOOM, so I can't provide twenty-four-hour security.*

"I believe there are measures we can take."

"How?"

It was embarrassing to ask my apprentice, but I hadn't even known about my own prowess for more than a month. If this were a new job, I'd still be in training, so there was no help for it.

"Let us use magic to cast a barrier."

"Can we do that? I don't have anything like that in my spell list."

I could use the following spells:

Teleportation, Levitation, Flame, Whirlwind, Item Appraisal, Earthquake, Ice and Snow, Lightning Attack, Mind Control, Break Spell, Detoxify, Reflect Spell, Mana Absorption, Language Comprehension, Transformation, Spell Creation.

There wasn't anything barrier related in there. At least, I didn't think there was.

"You had something called Spell Creation, didn't you? We can use that to create our own barrier."

*Create our own! We can do that? DIY. In this day and age, I guess even spells are homemade.*

"Is it that easy to make new spells? That's incredibly versatile."

"Ordinarily, it's impossible. For one thing, the spell for magic creation is ultra-advanced."

This had to be a level-99 thing.

"It's extraordinarily difficult to create a spell that does not exist, but it should be possible to create a barrier that will protect a city. Let's try it tomorrow."

Thanks to my apprentice, I'd learned something that hadn't even occurred to me before.

Taking her on might have been the right move.

We ate at the Savvy Eagle, the village restaurant, then retired to our new home.

The next day, Laika and I ventured to a high hill overlooking the village.

I say *ventured*, but we were very close to the house. I could actually see it from there.

"From here, I believe we'll be able to cover all directions."

Then Laika reverted to her dragon form and began scratching at the ground with her sharp claws.

At times like this, it was definitely more efficient to be a large dragon.

"Are you planning to till this area and plant a field?"

"I'm drawing a magic circle. Spells with long-term effects are more reliable if you use these."

"Oh, I see."

I'd begun using magic in earnest only a month ago, but since I'd been reading grimoires for a while, I did know the basics.

Attack spells and other magic with temporary effects tended to work even if your chant was off the cuff, and in certain situations, you could use them without chanting at all. You didn't need magic circles.

In other words, it was okay to be a little sloppy with the temporary ones.

However, when casting spells like this barrier—which had to last a long time and maintain its effectiveness—it was best to use a magic circle.

It wasn't that they were certain to fail without a circle, but an effect meant to last half a year could end after only three days.

As I hadn't been aware I could use a variety of spells, I hadn't memorized the details of how to draw magic circles, but given Laika was drawing the hexagon typical for defense spells, that was probably what this was.

"Still, you dragons know a lot about magic, too, don't you...?"

"If your life is three hundred years long, it's a waste to spend it lazing around. That's why I ended up studying magic in an attempt to improve myself, although I don't even use it."

"What, you're a poser?!"

In three centuries, I had never once thought of cultivating myself.

Possibly as a reaction to my history of slaving away, I'd developed the mind-set that what was important in life was relaxation.

Plus, back when I belonged to the company, work had been the only thing on my mind, and I'd never managed to take it easy. If I had, I wouldn't have ended up working myself to death.

"Now that I think about it, though, perhaps I should have spent that time habitually killing slimes or other similar monsters. On some level, I was proud, and I neglected to accrue experience."

"True, once your strength reaches a certain level, you don't even feel like fighting."

That was probably true for human adventurers as well.

I couldn't imagine level 50s went around killing petty slimes. They probably only fought heavyweights like dragons.

That said, battles with the big shots almost never happened. They might occur about as often as a festival, maybe even less than once a year.

As a result, levels plateaued at a certain point.

On top of that, as a rule, your body responds well only during a limited window of time in your life, so as people age, they grow weaker.

As far as that went, not only had I maintained the appearance and physical age of a seventeen-year-old, I'd killed slimes routinely, so the buildup had been enormous.

"All right, the magic circle is complete."

Yes, unless you were the size of a dragon, it would be completely impractical to make such an enormous magic circle.

"So I just stand in the center of this and chant?"

There were some exceptions, but that was usually what it took to activate them.

"I think that will do it. Now, come up with a chant as cool as you!"

My apprentice hit me with a ridiculous request.

Laika and I had talked it over beforehand and decided what sort of barrier it should be.

It was fairly advanced, but since I was level 99, I had confidence it would go well.

"Ye with wicked hearts, may this net ensnare you and rob you of freedom. As if by its own will, it shall fall on thee… HAAAAAaaaaaah!"

I felt as if power was pouring out of me from my head to my toes. A golden light flew toward the town, enveloped it—and winked out.

"Did that work?"

"Something infused with your wishes flew toward the village, Lady Azusa, so it will be fine."

If my apprentice says it'll be okay, no doubt it will be.

By the way, the barrier I'd cast had a couple of effects.

First, it covered the village with a magic shield. This way, if an attack spell came in from far away, we'd be able to block it. That was how normal barriers worked.

The other effect was something original.

If people with malicious hearts entered the village, the barrier would detect them and wrap around them like a net, immobilizing them.

Apparently, clerics who worked at shrines were able to use spells that trapped evildoers, and I'd combined one of those with this spell.

"To be honest, there's almost no precedent for giving a single magic barrier multiple effects. It was possible because you used Spell Creation, Lady Azusa, and because you are a witch of the highest order."

Laika was heaping on the praise so much that it was a little embarrassing.

"Since I've accrued so much power, I'll have to use it for good."

I'd skated along for three centuries, but I had taken care of the village.

The reason was simple: This was my home turf.

I made my home in the highlands, but I'd lived alongside the residents of this nearby hamlet, and the villagers thought so as well. If Flatta disappeared, I wouldn't be able to live by myself in that mountain house. The village of Flatta was like the nearest town with a train station.

I wanted to be useful to the place where I lived, at least. That had been my motive for making medicines and why I'd treated sick people.

For three hundred years, that had been my reason for being, the thing that gave value to my existence.

This barrier was in line with that perspective, so I'd cast it right away.

If I managed to protect the village, it would make me happy and give meaning to my accidental ascension to level 99.

It did seem that I might start getting requests to go save other villages and towns after this, which raised concerns about the future, but…

"All right. Let's return to the village and report this to the chief."

"In that case, please ride on my back."

"No, I'll walk this time."

I'd eaten quite a bit yesterday and wanted to get my exercise in.

When we explained the matter to the village chief, he was so happy he cried.

Enormous tears streamed down his face, so much so that I started worrying he would get dehydrated.

"That's splendid! You really do think about Flatta, great Witch of the Highlands!"

"It's just that I've heard that news of my strength is getting around, and I wanted to take precautions. I can't say that someone who takes pride in their own prowess won't do something to the village."

Say someone challenged me, the way Laika had, and I accepted and won. I couldn't guarantee the loser wouldn't strike at the village in a bid for revenge.

It was probably also true that, because of me, the name of Flatta was becoming more well-known. That increased the odds of troublemakers showing up.

"No, no! The concern that the village's security might be weak has come up on the agenda frequently over the past five hundred years. Now, at last, the problem is solved!"

*If it's been an issue that long, just do something about it already!*

Still, people tend to avoid taking safety measures until they get burned. They're generally stingy with the budget until then, too. Nobody wants to sink money into something that might turn out to be nothing.

"Why don't we erect a copper statue of you, great Witch?! I wager all the villagers would agree to it!"

"Whatever you do, please don't."

Someone who craved the limelight might have been happy with such an honor, but the idea left me completely cold.

Since we'd finished with the subject of the barrier, Laika and I returned to the remodeled house.

The problem with this type of security system is that it's hard to tell how well it's working when things are peaceful. It's like how you don't need doctors while you're healthy. If you want to see if a doctor is good, you need to be sick or injured.

That said, it would be best if things stayed so quiet that we'd never get to find out.

◇

So. We'd finished the day's real business, but there was still something I had to check.

Laika's cooking.

Since the two of us would be living together, we'd need to share the cooking and cleaning.

Preferably, I wanted my apprentice to shoulder most of it.

That said, if I left all of it to her, I'd risk rotting as a human being, so I planned to do a good bit of work myself. The goal was fifty-fifty.

However, if Laika's cooking was irredeemably awful, fifty-fifty wouldn't work. To that end, today, I was holding a test.

"First and foremost, do dragons even cook?"

You'd think they'd just gobble things down raw.

"Yes. After all, we aren't barbarians. Dragons are a noble race. We cook properly." Laika puffed out her chest.

"I've purchased a good array of groceries. Make something with them, all right?"

"Yes, I understand. I'll do my very best!"

Laika went into the kitchen, seeming pretty enthusiastic.

In this world, they have metal tanks filled with Flame magic, and it's possible to use them to adjust fires. However, they're luxury items, so they tend to be utilized only by the rich. The more frugal use stones that you can strike together to create sparks and set dry straw alight.

If you can use Flame magic, you do. Ever since I'd learned I could use it, I'd stuck to that method. Fire is very versatile, so magicians try to learn it first.

Laika exhaled a small stream of fire breath, as if she were whispering.

*I see... She can use flames even when she's in her girl form.*

"Okay, that's a good amount of fire. No problems at the moment. Calm down, calm down... I am a dragon... I'm not a woman to be perturbed over something like this."

*She does seem pretty flustered. Is she going to be okay?*

It's worth noting I was only overhearing her.

I'd decided not to look at what she was making. If I watched the whole time, I might have made her nervous, and I wouldn't have been able to anticipate whatever food she brought out.

About thirty minutes later...

...I heard a cheerful voice announce, "It's finished!"

Now then, what exactly had she cooked up?

The first plate held a large salad.

Some medicinal herbs were only faintly bitter and could be eaten either raw or boiled. Several of those were incorporated.

What drew the eye more than anything was—the enormous omelet on another plate.

She must have used about ten eggs.

"I do like omelets, but this one might have too many calories, don't you think?"

"It's my ultimate masterpiece. Go on—try it!"

Well, the issue of portion sizes was secondary. What really mattered was the flavor.

I took the first bite.

"...Oh! It's delicious!"

What a superb fluffy, silky texture!

"And you've filled it with sautéed onions and carrots?"

That part was standard. Even so, at this size, if the whole thing was that flavor, I could get tired of it— *Huh? It tastes different now!*

"Oh, if you go a little to the side, there's cheese, too!"

"That's right. I added small portions of different flavors to the omelet. It makes finding out what's underneath the egg a little more fun."

"Still, I'm surprised you managed to make such a huge omelet."

"When I went back to get the money, I picked up my cooking utensils and things as well."

She was that eager to become an apprentice? By now, I was appreciating her enthusiasm.

*Laika, girl, you're pretty good.*

The huge omelet was made so that you could enjoy a grand total of four different flavors. It was a lot like one of those giant rice balls with different fillings in different areas.

"Frankly, this is fantastic. I've only seen the omelet and the salad, but I'll acknowledge that you do indeed have cooking skills."

"Thank you very much! I'll continue to do my very best!"

Laika seemed thrilled at the praise.

My apprentice knew how to take a compliment about something perfectly normal, and I was grateful for the chance to offer them properly. It was a win-win relationship.

"The only thing is, I do think you might have used too many eggs… Maybe pay a little more attention to balance, all right?"

"My apologies. When I cook, my values as a dragon stay with me no matter what I do."

"Isn't your appetite the same as a human's when you're in your girl form?"

She didn't seem to have eaten all that much at the restaurant.

"I can get by with smaller servings than I could as a dragon, but those portions really don't seem like enough. They make me feel as if I'm dieting."

Even an omelet this enormous must have seemed pretty low-cal to a dragon.

"From now on, go ahead and order without holding back, all right?"

I felt like I was at risk of a little heartburn, so I drank some medicine that was good for the digestive system. It was made entirely from herbs, so I didn't have to worry about how much I took.

—And just then, I felt something like a premonition.

"That's weird... I think something just happened in the village."

"Do you suppose the barrier has been triggered?"

True, we had set up the barrier that day, and it might have been why I felt ill. In all of my three hundred years, I'd never experienced this before.

That being the case, it made sense to go check.

"Laika, we're going to the village."

"Yes, ma'am!"

Laika had switched to her dragon form, and I rode through the night sky on her back.

As always, she changed to her girl form just outside the village. Then she went in with me.

From a distance, I could see people lighting a bonfire.

That meant something had happened.

"Excuse me. What's going on?"

"Oh, it's the great Witch and her apprentice!"

"You came right away!"

Amid the uproar, the village chief, who'd already arrived, explained...

...though I knew roughly what to expect, thanks to the man lying hogtied on the ground.

"A man came to the village after nightfall, and he suddenly couldn't move."

That must have been the bound man.

"When we asked around, we learned that he's a wanted thief who's been plundering the province lately. I expect he pilfered in a nearby town and then drifted into our village."

"The barrier worked, then?"

"That's right. It's all thanks to you, great Witch!"

*I see: So the power over malicious people works on thieves, too.*

"I was scoping out the tavern from the back door, thinking I'd steal something, and all of a sudden, I couldn't move. What the hell is this?" the culprit confessed. "I was going to filch something from the tavern, then make my getaway during the night."

Then the barrier had indeed responded to clearly wicked intent.

"That's wonderful, Lady Azusa. It worked immediately!" Laika was happy, too.

"True, it did prove useful to the village."

Regardless, I didn't deserve all the praise here. I wanted to keep things fair.

"Residents of Flatta, my apprentice, Laika, was the one who suggested this barrier. Please express your gratitude to her as well!"

I patted Laika's back, giving her a push.

The villagers liked doling out compliments, and their eyes turned to Laika.

"I knew the great Witch's apprentice would be different."

"Having a dragon with a good heart here is like having a hundred more people on our side!"

"This village is gonna be a real comfortable place to live!"

*Yep, that's right. I'm proud of my student—bring on the praise.*

"N-no, Lady Azusa is the one who created this barrier... I really didn't do any..."

Laika seemed embarrassed, but if she was going to be my apprentice, she'd have to get used to this as well.

"This is rather awkward, isn't it...?"

"It doesn't feel terrible, though, does it?"

My educational policy is "foster growth through praise."

Why? Because when I was a wage slave, no one ever had a kind word for me. They ran me ragged, and the frustration built up.

I'd spent only five years in that environment, but even after three hundred years as a witch, those memories were still clear as day.

As a rule, people like being complimented.

In education, it might be bad to do nothing but praise people, but I'd like to give accolades whenever I can. If that generates enthusiasm, that's a very good thing, isn't it?

At any rate, there had been no damage to the village, and I was really glad about that.

And with that relief came a yawn.

"Well then, we'll take our leave. Sleep well."

"Um…if you would like, you may spread the word that your village is under the protection of a dragon. Lady Azusa loves this village, and I will defend it as well… Now, if you'll excuse me."

Laika and I returned to our house in the highlands.

"Lady Azusa, since the barrier activated slightly, it might be best to recast it tomorrow."

"That sounds like a pain…"

After that, word traveled that a witch had created a barrier to protect the village of Flatta.

I'd managed to contribute to the peace of the village, and I considered it an honor.

Since we'd solved the problem of the barrier, I began Laika's lessons in earnest.

That said, there was really nothing I could teach her.

I wandered around the highlands with Laika in her girl form.

If we encountered a slime, I killed it and retrieved the magic stone immediately.

That was it.

I did, however, move fast. The moment a slime entered my field of vision, my hands were already moving.

I'd poke the lowly monster quickly with a finger. That was all it took for the slime to expire and vanish.

I took its magic stone and put it in my bag.

"Amazing! Your movements were so quick that I couldn't follow them with my eyes!"

"I may not look it, but I have been killing slimes for three centuries, you know."

When it came to slime slaying, I was most definitely first-class... Although, it was doubtful whether that was something to brag about.

"After you've killed slimes for a while, your body starts reacting and killing them automatically. Once that happens, I'm sure your level will begin rising rapidly."

"I understand. I'll work hard so that, someday, I'll be able to stand on equal footing with you, Lady Azusa!"

As she said this, she spotted a slime, thrust out a hand, and knocked it away.

Laika's attack power was significant, so she could kill them with a light bump from her hands or feet.

"By the way, Lady Azusa, approximately how many slimes did you kill each day?"

"Um, let's see. About twenty-five? Oh, but I had an effect that increased the number of experience points I acquire, so practically speaking, I suppose it would be about fifty."

Well, it wasn't likely that I'd just barely reached level 99 when I checked (after all, even after you hit level 99, your total experience points would keep increasing), so I thought there was probably a more accurate number. I just didn't know what it was.

"Even fifty seems surprisingly easy. I just assumed you'd put in backbreaking effort..."

It was fair to say it hadn't been much work at all.

"Listen, though, if it had been backbreaking, I couldn't have kept it up for three hundred years. If you do something anyone can do way more than anyone else ever does it, there's meaning in that."

Putting it that way was like claiming I'd done something meaningful, which was a little embarrassing.

"I see! I'd expect no less from you, Lady Azusa! What profound words!"

Not only that, but Laika was deeply moved, which made it even more awkward.

*Still, there might be at least some wisdom in my choices. As a teacher, maybe I should tell her about that.*

"Say, Laika, you mentioned 'backbreaking effort,' but get rid of that idea, all right?"

"Huh? Why is that?"

Maybe my words seemed paradoxical to her. Laika looked perplexed.

"You see, people put in backbreaking effort on the assumption that someone will see it. When you used that expression, you were probably at least a little proud of it."

"N-now that you mention it…"

When you go through excruciating effort or training, you start feeling impressive for having done it.

To a certain extent, it's unavoidable.

Frankly, when I was owned by the company, I'd tried to consider myself notable for my efforts, too.

I'd also believed, unconsciously, that I was better than the more easygoing types or the unemployed.

That, however, had been a big mistake.

"Listen, Laika. If you do something because you want people to think you're so great, and then they don't, you won't be able to endure it, or you'll lose your enthusiasm. I was able to keep this up for as long as I did because I never thought about how people would see me."

"What profound wisdom…!"

Laika was listening very intently.

"I do things because I like them and because I want to do them. If you feel that way about something, you'll be able to stick with it. Do you understand?"

"I really am glad I chose you as my teacher, Lady Azusa. The scales have fallen from my eyes! You mean if I want to grow stronger, I must discard the desire to have others think well of me! Since I am improving myself, I should face myself first... How insightful! What a deep, meaningful doctrine!"

I didn't think I'd said anything that grand.

*It's fine to be impressed, but don't go getting disillusioned on me later.*

That day, I ended the training when Laika had eliminated about sixty slimes.

"It's not like the slimes will ever take revenge, so be sure to kill them steadily."

I lived to regret that remark.

Why do I always end up saying things that trigger a flag?

# AZUSA AIZAWA

The protagonist. Commonly known as "the Witch of the Highlands." A girl (?) who was reincarnated as an unaging, undying witch with the body of a seventeen-year-old. Since she died of overwork in our world, she's especially sensitive to labor conditions.

WHEN IT'S TIME TO REST, YOU REST. DON'T MAKE A VIRTUE OF WORKING TOO MUCH!

# LAIKA

A dragon girl apprenticed to Azusa, "the Witch of the Highlands." She's about three hundred years old. She was originally proud of her strength, but since Azusa defeated her, she's turned over a new leaf. She's conscientious, very serious, and cares a lot about what people think.

I WANT TO STUDY MORE TO IMPROVE MYSELF!

My peace had been threatened for a few days after my first contact with Laika, but the waters had calmed again.

In other words, I'd gotten used to sharing my home.

There was plenty of room in the house, so we could both have some time and space to ourselves. We also took turns doing the cooking, cleaning, and shopping, which made things easier on both of us.

Because we were teacher and apprentice, our relationship wasn't equal, but for joint living, it was ideal.

Long ago, when I'd lived in Japan, room sharing had been fairly popular.

If you included friends of friends, I'd known several people with roommates.

The bottom line, though, was that I frequently heard about how hard it was.

The primary challenge was it was exhausting living with someone whose values were too different from your own. The sense of distance was difficult as well.

I'd heard about someone with a roommate who sent them texts and Line messages over every little thing, and when the messages were ignored for a short while, the roommate ripped the person a new one and left.

Life with someone lacking in common sense or public decency can be a trial, too.

It's tough when your roommate always skips the cleaning when it's their turn. Even if doing someone else's chores isn't actually that bad, wondering why you're doing it takes a hefty psychological toll.

I'd heard many other reports of trouble, so for a long time—more than three hundred years, at least—I'd believed that having my own place couldn't be beat.

But if your roommate is considerate, things work out. I could tell, living with Laika.

She also said things like "There's much I can learn from you, Lady Azusa" practically every day, so I guess the arrangement was worthwhile.

What I was actually doing for Laika was anyone's guess, but excellent apprentices have the ability to find their teachers' good points without any help.

On top of that, she'd rescued me a bit.

I hadn't confirmed this directly, but apparently, news that the Witch of the Highlands had defeated a dragon had spread over all of Nanterre, at the very least. The story that the dragon had become my apprentice was traveling, too.

I'd thought that might provoke a big spike in attempts to take my dojo, but by all appearances, it had done the opposite.

Adventurers who already knew they were no match for a dragon had decided not to bother trying at all.

Thanks to that, I was enjoying a pretty peaceful life.

On days when Laika did the cleaning, I could use that time to relax and read grimoires.

It reminded me of certain memories from my previous life.

To be precise, it reminded me of lying in my room reading comics and magazines while my mother cleaned.

Yes, that indolent time when even corporate slaves were released from their servitude: visiting home.

Now that I had a roommate, those blissful spells—or something like them—became an almost-everyday reality!

Since I'd lived alone for so long, I'd forgotten this pleasure.

Well, things truly didn't get better than this. Long live room sharing!

Of course, on days when it was my turn, I cleaned. I wouldn't throw my weight around just because I was the teacher.

As a matter of fact, I was well aware I wasn't big and important enough to do that.

I wanted Laika to experience what it was like to have your mom do everything during a trip home, too.

At any rate, despite the public revelation that I was level 99, I was managing to maintain my idyllic life.

*I wish this peace would last forever...*

Oh. That was a flag, wasn't it? One of those thoughts you just shouldn't think.

*Bam-bam, bam-bam.*

Someone knocked on the door.

*Who could it be? This house doesn't often get visitors.*

"Shall I answer it?"

"No, you go ahead and clean, Laika. I'll get it."

I closed my grimoire and headed for the entryway.

When I opened the door, the individual standing there was a girl with blue hair. She looked to be about ten years old.

Even in this world, I didn't remember seeing many people with blue hair.

Her expression was cheerful, and her eyes were sparkling as they fixed on me.

At the very least, she didn't seem to be lost.

"Hello. Did you need something?"

Since the visitor hadn't been an adventurer about to say "Fight me!" my expression softened.

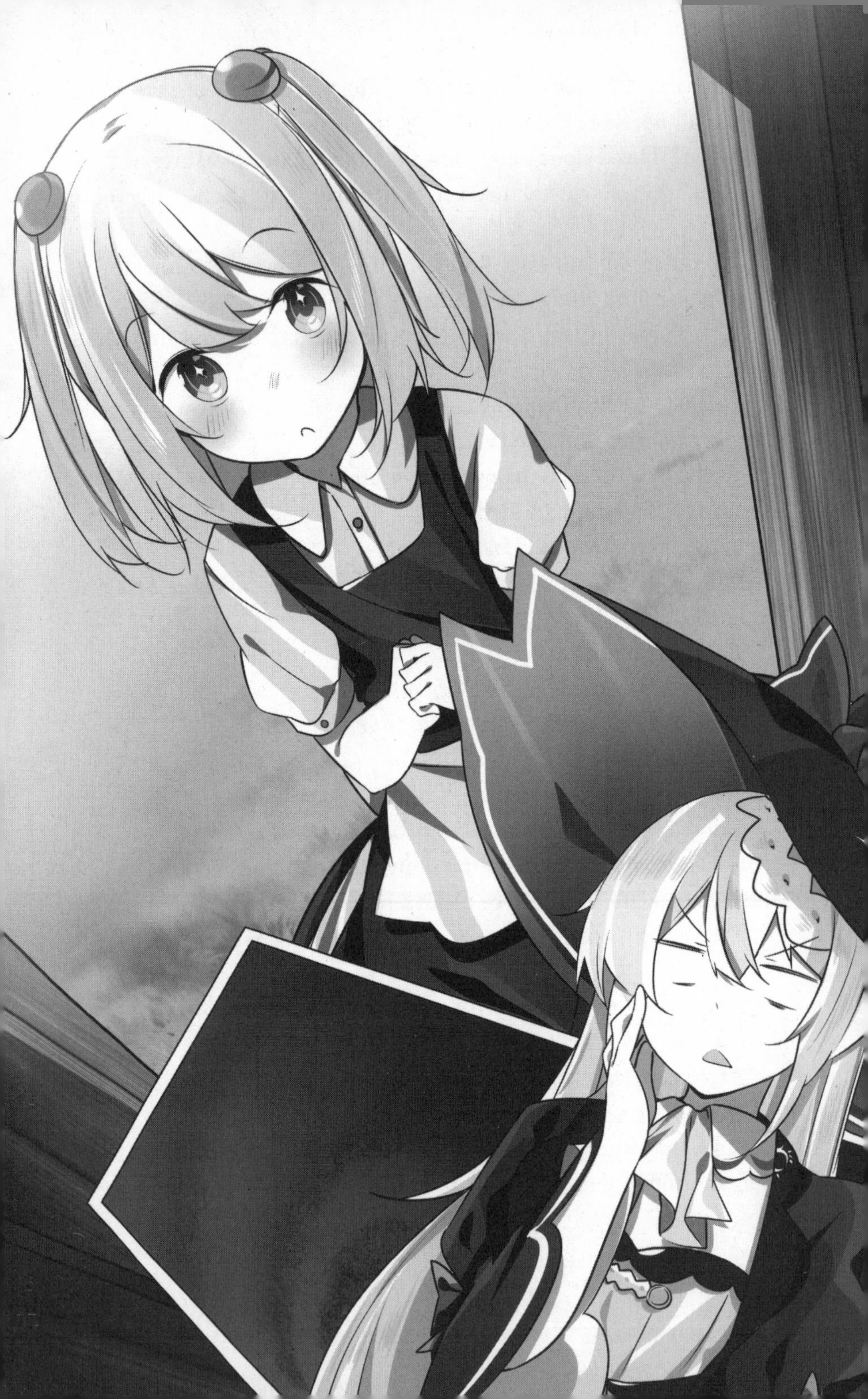

The highlands around here were peaceful, and children probably played nearby sometimes.

"I finally got to see you! I'm so happy!"

*What's this? Am I popular with children now, too?*

"I'm so glad to meet you, Mommy!"

I turned to stone.

Just so you know, I don't mean that someone hit me with a Petrification spell. It was a figure of speech.

*Mommy? Did this girl say mommy?*

"Um…I'm not your mommy, dear. I'm pretty sure you're looking for somebody else."

"Huh? No, that can't be. You're Falfa's mommy, Mommy. Falfa knows for sure."

A girl I'd just met was calling me her mother.

Good thing she hadn't said it in the village. That would have been sure to start unwanted rumors. Not only that, but the village being what it was, those rumors would have spread fast.

For the record, in my three hundred years in this world, I'd never had a real romantic relationship.

There was a good reason.

I was an immortal witch, and even if I fell in love with somebody, they'd get old and die without me.

It was hard enough watching the villagers die. A lover would have been too painful.

For that reason, I'd consciously steered clear of romance.

Definitely not because I wasn't popular or anything. Seriously.

On top of that, the only people I had much contact with were the villagers.

As far as they were concerned, I was a witch who'd been there since long before they were born, like the village's guardian deity. They might feel awe and respect for me, but romantic love probably didn't seem like an option.

…And so, that sort of love had never been a part of my life.

Naturally, I had no children.

"Your name is Falfa?"

"Uh-huh. Falfa."

"Falfa, 'Mommy' is what you call the lady who gave birth to you and raised you. You don't call other women 'Mommy.'"

She probably just defined the word *mommy* differently than the rest of the world.

"That's not true. You made me, Mommy."

……

*Well, this is strange…*

*I can't possibly have forgotten going through childbirth.*

"Lady Azusa, who in the world is it?"

Apparently of the opinion that I was taking a long time to deal with this, Laika had left off cleaning and come over.

"I'm Falfa. I came to meet Mommy."

"Lady Azusa, you have a child?!"

"No, I don't. This girl has the wrong idea."

"Falfa doesn't have the wrong idea."

"Lady Azusa, is it possible you're a stepmother?"

This had become so complicated that I was getting confused.

I'd been prepared for adventurers trying to best me, but this ordeal was too new.

"I even know you're called the Witch of the Highlands. My little sister looked it up."

"You have a little sister?!"

*So now I'm the mother of at least two daughters. What's going on here?*

"And you see, Mommy, my little sister's trying to kill you, so I thought I should let you know, and that's why I'm here."

"She wants to kill me?!"

*And now we're suddenly in a thriller...*

"I don't want you to die, Mommy. That's why I came here before she did. To warn you."

Falfa's expression had hardened. She didn't appear to be joking, and she didn't seem mature enough to pull a prank like this anyway.

"Lady Azusa, for now, let's invite the child in and listen to what she has to say."

Laika was right. This was way too creepy.

"Falfa, I'll give you some sweets. Come on in."

"Sure! Falfa wants sweets!"

"In exchange, would you explain more about what you just told me?"

"Uh-huh! Uh-huh!"

Falfa nodded energetically.

*Did she resemble me as a child, just a little...? —Nope. Not really.*

I'd baked cookies two days earlier, so I had Laika retrieve them.

While we waited, the girl and I continued our conversation in the living room.

"What is your little sister's name, Falfa?"

"Shalsha."

"And Shalsha is my child, too?"

"Mm-hmm, that's right."

I felt like I was grilling a witness. Still, my life was on the line, so...

Here's what I knew at this point:

I had another daughter named Shalsha, and she was gunning for me.

In other words, almost nothing. I'd have to get a lot more information out of her.

"Do you know why Shalsha is after me?"

"I think it's because she resents you, Mommy. I bet she's mad because you killed her."

*This is weird.*

My laid-back fantasy life had taken a sharp turn for the sci-fi.

I had daughters I didn't remember giving birth to, and on top of that, one of them was trying to get revenge on me for killing her.

Was there even a logical explanation for this bizarre twist of events?

Just then, Laika came in, carrying a plate of cookies.

Falfa squealed, "Yaaaay, cookies!" and innocently began chowing down.

"I could hear the two of you back there. In any case, we will need to protect you from this Shalsha individual, won't we?"

"That would be a top priority, yes."

Finding out who the enemy really was would come later.

"Falfa, do you know how she will attack?"

"Shalsha spent a long, loooong time training with the Smiting Evil spell."

Smiting Evil was a spell that exercised great power against a specific race, and only that race.

For example, one could negate attacks from humans, orcs, or elves and inflict damage on them.

People who acquired such magic often ended up as expert race-specific assassins known by aliases like "Cyclops Killer" or "Specter Slayer."

The narrower its focus, the more powerful Smiting Evil's effect, and the thinner it was spread, the weaker it got. For example, a spell like Smiting Evil (Living Creature) would do almost nothing. Not that anyone was likely to try learning that.

"A Smiting Evil spell, hmm? They say even high-level casters have to spend decades on it before it's worth anything."

I knew what Laika meant. It was why people became expert race-specific assassins.

The spell took so long to acquire that it wasn't a sought-after skill.

For that reason, if Shalsha'd only lived as long as her elder sister's apparent age suggested, her Smiting Evil spell would probably be limited in power... But both Laika and I had been alive for three centuries, so I couldn't bank on that.

"How old is Shalsha?"

"Um, maybe fifty?"

Falfa tilted her head as she spoke. Maybe she wasn't very confident in her answer.

Still, working from that, I could guess.

The enemy was either immortal or something like it.

In that case, there was a risk she'd be a caster to watch out for.

But what iteration of Smiting Evil would work against me? Smiting Evil (Human)? Or would it be Smiting Evil (Immortal)?

"I bet Shalsha's gonna be here soon. Be careful, Mommy."

Falfa was eating a cookie as she spoke, and right after that, it happened.

*Clatter, clatter, clatter...* The window glass trembled.

I had a bad feeling about whatever was out there!

"I'm going to check outside."

Growing uneasy, I left the house.

Laika and Falfa followed me.

Standing far off in the highlands was a little girl who looked a lot like Falfa.

Her hair was light green, though, and it was floating slightly.

"Shalsha finally found you, Witch of the Highlands...," the girl called in a resounding voice.

"Shalsha! Don't pick on Mommy!"

Falfa calling this girl by name positively identified her as Shalsha.

"Be quiet, Sister. I am going to avenge my murder."

Yep, she was talking like she'd been killed.

"Shalsha, wasn't it? I don't think I can possibly have killed you. What is this about?"

Shalsha snorted. "Hey, just how many slimes do you think you've killed?"

*Huh? Why are we talking about slimes now?*

"My sister and I were born from the assembled souls of slaughtered slimes. We're slime spirits!"

"Slime spirits!!!!!!!"

*I would understand flame spirits or water spirits, but are slime spirits even a thing?!*

"That's right. You destroyed an astronomical number of slimes in this area, and their minuscule souls accumulated until they created slime spirits, beings without precedent—my sister and I!"

Shalsha sounded bitter.

"As a result, the anger of the countless lives you stole dwells in Shalsha, too. I've come to balance the scales."

I'd assumed it was impossible for the slimes to take revenge, but apparently, I'd been incorrect.

I'd created an enemy...

"All right. Fight me. I'll kill you and offer you to the souls of the slimes to ensure their repose."

"'Ensure their repose'? But didn't those souls get together and turn into you?"

It was kinda like they'd been recycled (?), in a way...

"Shut up, shut up! Come at me."

She looked more miffed than enraged, but she was definitely planning to go through with this.

"Lady Azusa, why not hit her with a whirlwind and see what happens?" Laika suggested.

"Well, she is a spirit. I doubt I would have to worry about it killing her... You're right. Maybe I'll do that."

I thrust a hand out in front of me.

Then I unleashed a tempest at Shalsha.

However—

"Vanish, whirlwind."

—at the girl's command, the attack did indeed disappear.

"You see, I trained for many, many years and obtained the spell Smiting Evil (Witch of the Highlands). That means I'll never lose to you."

"Y-y-y-you what?!"

*I—I see...* The narrower the range of Smiting Evil, the more powerful it was. If the spell was limited to me specifically, it would be a force to be reckoned with.

But was it even possible to learn a spell targeting someone you'd only just met?

"As slime spirits, the two of us understood why we were born. For that reason, my sister Shalsha investigated places where many slimes had been killed, tracked you down, then gathered fallen hairs and other materials she needed for Smiting Evil," Falfa told me.

So the same premise as putting hair inside a doll to curse somebody...

"I wanted to meet you sooner, Mommy, but Shalsha said we mustn't meet our enemy... When her Smiting Evil spell was complete, though, I couldn't just leave things this way, so I came here."

"You're such a good girl, Falfa!"

"Well, you're my mommy, Mommy."

It was complicated, but they had been born because of me, so you could probably say I was their mother.

Was this the result of my abnormal focus on killing slimes?

"By the way, Falfa, don't you hate me?"

"I'm a spirit born from the assembled souls of slimes, but I want to be friends with you, Mommy, because I got to be born at all."

She was this close to triggering my maternal instincts. Such an incredibly good girl...

However, this wasn't the time for that.

Little by little, Shalsha was approaching.

"How strange. My sister and I were born at the same time, so why are our personalities so very different? I can't forgive the Witch of the Highlands."

That sinister atmosphere was spreading.

"To be frank, Smiting Evil (Witch of the Highlands) is an extremely unique spell, and the amount of mana it consumes is vast. Even if I invest fifty years' worth of mana, it will last only a few hours. And it was all for this day..."

*Talk about lousy mileage!*

"There must have been a more normal way for you to live! Did you really just sit around and wait all that time without taking revenge?"

"When I was born fifty years ago, you were already one of the most powerful witches in existence. I could tell from how fast you were exterminating slimes. That was why I decided to develop an exclusive spell and store up mana."

She'd clearly poured her passion into the wrong thing.

"Use any spell you like. Every one of them will be rendered powerless!"

This time, I tried hitting her with fire.

"Red flames, blue flames, black flames! Serve as my strength!"

Fire blazed up, bright and crimson, and hit Shalsha with a merciless blast.

…But she was completely unscathed. The inferno seemed to fly apart before reaching her.

"Now do you see the power of Smiting Evil (Witch of the Highlands)?"

Shalsha didn't strike me as the expressive type, but now she wore a fearless smile.

"This is bad…"

If none of my attacks had any effect, I had no way to fight.

In that case—was running my only option?

When something's hurting you, get out of there.

In my previous life, my work had killed me because I couldn't escape my corporate servitude.

This time, I was going to run for it!

I had a Levitation spell.

I'd heard this spell would last only for a few hours, so if I managed to keep running until then, I could deal with it!

I rose into the air.

However, when I was about ten meters off the ground—

"O spell, vanish," Shalsha murmured, and I dropped to the ground with a thud.

My feet throbbed.

"That's not safe… If I weren't a level-99 witch, I could have broken something."

"I won't let you get away. I'm going to kill you like all the slimes *you've* killed."

Shalsha was slowly coming closer.

Was it… Was it time to pay the piper?

Even if I was level 99, how could I win when my opponent was like an ultimate weapon designed to defeat me? Besides, I'd already lived for three centuries.

"Falfa, sweetheart, I'm glad I met you before the end."

Falfa was nearby, and I hugged her tightly.

Embracing my daughter before my imminent death—poignant, don't you think?

"Mommy! Don't say things like that! Help Falfa think of a way out!" Falfa was shouting. *I'm sorry. It looks like there's nothing I can do, though.*

"Lady Azusa! Leave this to me!"

Laika was desperate, too.

"Thank you, Laika. I was proud to have you as my apprentice. Also, your omelets were delicious."

"It's all right! We can win!"

"Stop it… There's no way we can beat that. You'll get hurt, Laika!"

"It's just as she says. I only intend to kill the Witch of the Highlands. I don't plan to go after anyone else, so hurry and run away."

I remembered a horror movie I'd seen a long time ago. A machine-like assassin creeping ever closer. Just like this…

Still, she sure was taking her time. She wasn't trying to end this fight in one go.

"My little sister is a slow runner," little Falfa suggested.

"Doesn't that mean we could get away if we ran…?"

Laika seemed to have heard.

She'd transformed from girl to dragon and planted herself before Shalsha in confrontation.

"I won't allow you to take a single step beyond this point!"

"Out of my way, dragon." Shalsha's voice was cold.

"I refuse! I have a duty to protect my teacher!"

"Don't! Laika, that's dangerous!"

Laika turned her head toward me slightly and smiled. "It's all right, Lady Azusa. I'll catch up with you right away, so please run!"

"That's like guaranteeing you'll die!"

*I'm telling you, don't even go there! I know you won't actually catch up!*

"You see, my elder sister is getting married next month. I must attend her wedding."

"Why are you making this worse?!"

"I'll protect you, Lady Azusa! Eat this! Dragon Kick!"

Laika's foot lashed out at Shalsha.

It was hopeless... I knew how it would go. Her target would win with a counterattack.

But it never came.

"Uu... Ow... It hurts..."

Shalsha had fallen.

*Huh? This isn't what I was expecting.*

Laika was cautiously examining her opponent.

"Lady Azusa, she's unconscious. I won."

"Huh?! You can win with a twist like that?!"

She had derailed the cliché.

"My sister, Shalsha, overspecialized in magic that would kill you, Mommy, so I guess she's really weak against everybody else."

Falfa spoke the truth.

Ah. Laika was a dragon, so Shalsha's spell hadn't affected her.

Now that the matter was settled, I mused:

"Shalsha's kind of an...awkward child..."

After Laika's attack knocked Shalsha out, my crisis was over for the time being.

We couldn't just leave her lying on the ground, so I put her to bed in an empty room in my house.

We'd furnished the rooms with guest beds for times like this.

An hour later, Shalsha woke up.

"Uhhh… Uuuhn… Where am I?"

"Oh, Shalsha's awake!"

Falfa rushed over to her.

"Oh, Sister… Agh! The Witch of the Highlands is here!"

Laika and I were in the room, too.

"Laika beat you, and you collapsed, so we put you to bed."

"Your unwarranted mercy will be your doom. I have the spell Smiting Evil (Witch of the Highlands), and— Huh? My power…"

"You burned through all your mana, so you won't be able to use that for another several decades."

Shalsha's face blanched. She must have realized she couldn't activate her spell.

We'd heard about that from her sister Falfa and had already made sure.

After all, if she'd been able to use it for another hour, we'd have had problems.

"N-no… What was the point of my life up until now?"

"I really couldn't tell you. That's what happens when you live a tragic life of revenge. Honestly, I'd say you're lucky I'm alive."

"Wh-what do you mean?"

"If I'd died, your life really would have been meaningless. As long as I'm around, you can work toward your payback."

I thought that optimistic remark might have been laying it on a little thick, but Shalsha took it quite seriously.

"You could put it that way…"

"Yes, you see?"

Apparently, I'd managed to persuade her.

Shalsha glanced at her arm. It had medicinal herbs bound to it in lieu of a poultice.

"Mommy knows a whole lot about medicines!"

"You got hurt fighting Laika, you know. You should heal twice as fast this way… Though I don't know much about slime spirit recuperation."

"Witch of the Highlands, you'd go so far…?"

"Working with medicinal herbs is my job as a witch. If you're injured, I'll treat you."

"B-but can there be anything in it for you, Witch?"

The child certainly did ask a lot of questions.

"Well, I am your mother, aren't I? In that case, I can't very well leave you in that state."

Actually, if any child collapsed, I'd help them even if I weren't their parent. We're ignoring her actual age in this case.

Right now, though, I should probably admit I was doing it because I was her mother.

For some reason, Shalsha's eyes had filled with tears.

"Y-you could make the case that you are my parent. But… E-even so, you are the slimes' enemy, and…"

Falfa took Shalsha's hand.

"Shalsha, stop putting up a front, okay?"

"Sister…"

"Slimes and humans fight; that's just how it is. Even now, slimes are being killed all over the world. Mommy disappearing wouldn't change that."

True. On a global scale, the number of slimes I'd eradicated was probably infinitesimal.

"Never mind that. Let's think of a way to live happily. That's more fun, isn't it?"

Shalsha nodded in response.

Despite her childish bearing, Falfa was being a proper big sister.

"Lady Azusa, it looks as though this matter is settled."

Having watched the whole business from start to finish, Laika seemed relieved.

"You're right. I really wasn't sure how things were going to turn out this time, but…"

"Oh! Lady Azusa, if we split them into fourths, I think my omelets and other meals would be the perfect size for a typical appetite."

Her words were clearly intended to suggest the four of us have dinner together.

"But, Laika, a quarter wouldn't be enough for you…"

"I-I'll make extra for myself."

All right, I'd accept those good intentions.

I approached my daughters.

"We still have empty rooms, so if you'd like, you can live here. In fact, just c'mon and move in."

Where and how these two had been living was a mystery, but I could ask about that later.

"Sure! Falfa wants to live with you, Mommy!"

The older sister wouldn't be a problem.

Now, what about the younger one?

Shalsha seemed conflicted, but…

"Witch of the Highlands…"

"No calling me 'Witch of the Highlands.' Find something a little more familial."

After a moment, Shalsha averted her eyes and said—

"……M-Mom." She sounded as if she was going through her rebellious phase. "Shalsha…wouldn't mind living with you, either."

"Okay, then that settles it. Why don't we have a party today?!"

When you want to deepen a relationship, parties are a good place to start.

This would be nothing like the drinking parties I'd reluctantly attended ages ago.

"Maybe I'll make a tart."

"Yaaaay! I love tarts!" Falfa cheered.

"In that case, I'll make an omelet again."

"Yaaaay! I love omelets, too!"

It didn't take much to make this girl happy.

On the other hand, Shalsha looked sulky, but…

"Mom… I'll help with the cooking," she said without smiling.

"Yes, thank you. I believe I'll take you up on that."

Frankly, I didn't feel remotely guilty about killing slimes.

Besides, if you took that logic to the extreme, you wouldn't be able to kill any living things at all.

Humans eat living creatures for the most part, so if you wanted to avoid taking lives, you'd have to die.

Nevertheless, it was probably true that my slime slaying had led to the birth of these girls. In which case, I might be able to bring peace to the souls of the departed by acting as their mother.

Plus, I simply thought the girls needed one.

They'd probably managed to make do on their own, but it would be better for them to have a place to call home.

I'd spent an easygoing three hundred years as a witch in another world.

I'd killed slime after slime and acquired twin daughters as a result.

When you're long-lived, all sorts of things happen to you, don't they…?

A laid-back existence with a large family might be good in its own way.

"By the way, do slime spirits eat regular food?"

"We don't need to eat, but we can," Shalsha responded, still looking down.

We were gradually beginning to communicate.

"Oh…"

Laika's expression said she'd just noticed a problem. She spoke to Falfa, sounding apologetic.

"Um…is it all right if I kill slimes, in the future?"

"Sure! It's part of the laws of nature!"

"Don't trouble yourself about it."

Both sisters had okayed it, so it looked as though Laika would be able to continue her training.

After that, we set out the food, and I asked my daughters all kinds of questions about themselves.

Even though I was calling them my daughters, there was much I didn't know about them. If I was going to understand them, I had to ask.

First, where had they lived?

"In a hut in the forest," Shalsha answered. "My big sister and I were born in the woods, so we lived in a little place no one was using."

"And then we went to a nearby town? The director of an orphanage gave us money, and we used that to buy clothes and shoes and stuff."

"Since we were strong enough to work as adventurers, we did that to earn money."

"We lived for a month on one gold coin, didn't we?"

A humble but honest life, it seemed.

Next, what exactly was a slime spirit?

"We can stretch our hair out like tentacles. My hair is light green because of its slime-like properties."

"Mine is blue and my little sister's is green because we're spirits."

"We don't really have any other distinctive traits. Although, as spirits, we don't seem to have natural life spans."

"Uh-huh. We both just stay like this."

I'd gotten a general idea of what exactly they were.

"By the way, what sort of work did you do when you were adventurers?"

They didn't strike me as very strong. Had they been full-fledged adventurers and defeated monsters?

"We vanquished evil slimes."

*Say what?*

"You see, there are two types of slimes, good ones and bad ones."

*Meaning slimes are subject to the dichotomy of good and evil?*

"We killed the bad ones and sold them for two hundred gold each."

*That's the same as me!*

"We didn't kill any good slimes, of course. As far as Shalsha is concerned, there's no problem."

*I see. Apparently, you can't fight your blood heritage.*

Though, these girls were made of slimes, so we definitely weren't blood relations.

And so I figured I'd learned the essentials. I'd discover the rest in the course of our days together.

"All right, we have a few house rules. Make sure to follow them, you two!"

"Okaaay!"

Instead of speaking aloud, Shalsha simply nodded.

"First, when it's your turn to do chores, do them properly. I mean things like cleaning or working in the field."

"Okaaay!"

As before, Shalsha just nodded.

It would have felt odd coming up with a nickname or something for the enthusiastic Falfa but not Shalsha, so I decided I'd just call my daughters by their names.

"We'll get the chore chart figured out later. Other than that...was there anything else?"

I'd never had children before, so I didn't really know.

"Oh, right. If you haven't been to school at all, do you want me to teach you? Do you know how to write?"

"My big sister sneaked into the house of the town's scholar to read mathematics essays and stuff. The two of them really hit it off after that."

*I apologize for treating you like children.*

"My sister, Shalsha, is really good at history, theology, and geometry."

*I might be the one getting educated here...*

At this rate, my dignity as a mother wouldn't last. I had to do something, or my daughters would start underestimating me.

*All right, I'll let them see people respecting me.*

"There's a village called Flatta nearby. I'll show you around tomorrow. I owe them a lot, so make sure you're on your best behavior, you two."

This time, they both nodded.

◇

Laika, my two daughters, and I walked to the village of Flatta.

On the way, slimes blocked our path again, so I brushed them away.

At my current level, though, that was enough to dispose of them.

"Um, just to make sure, it really is okay to kill these guys…?"

To be on the safe side, I checked with my daughters.

"Sure. I never minded at all, and my little sister already seems used to it."

"Yes……Mom."

I was relieved to have permission.

Since we were a four-person family now, we needed to earn more magic stones and money than before.

"The slimes here are evil."

"Yes, I think so, too! Get rid of the bad slimes and purify the world!"

With these proclamations, my two daughters slaughtered some slimes themselves.

"So…you can tell if they're wicked? What do you look for?"

"If you see it, you'll understand."

With that, Shalsha abruptly dived into a thicket.

I could hear some scrambling around in the brush, and then she returned with a slime in hand.

"I noticed it lurking in there."

Apparently, she had expert slime-catching skills. I'd expect no less of a slime spirit.

"Look. As a rule, Nanterre slimes are a deeper color. But this one is pretty pale."

"I'd never heard that distinction before."

I'd never once paid attention to the color of slimes.

"They're pale because they're tainted by their evil hearts, so it's better to exterminate them."

"I-is that right...? That's very informative..."

"Slimes have a 'hole.' That's their weak point. Poke them there, and they'll die instantly."

"A hole? But slimes don't have anything like that."

Falfa lightly jabbed the one Shalsha was holding.

"This slime is already deaaad!"

The creature blinked out of existence.

"See?"

I get the feeling it's precisely because they're former slimes that they show their kind no mercy.

"That's incredible. I must learn to kill slimes like that myself..."

"Laika, you're welcome to be impressed, but there's nothing wrong with just taking care of them the regular way, all right?"

It's not like you get more experience points for style.


As we chatted, we reached Flatta.

Today's objective was the public presentation of my daughters.

Just so you know, I did plan to tell people they were slime spirits.

The two of them seemed to have a few unique powers, and I thought it best to let people know ahead of time.

However, things kept getting complicated again.

The first time was when we were passing by the greengrocer's at the village entrance.

"Oh, Mommy, there's all kinds of fruit for sale!" Falfa called cheerfully.

The lady who ran the shop heard her.

"What?! Great Witch, you have children?! Not only that, but...are they twins?!"

*Mm-hmm, that's about the reaction I was expecting...*

"Yes, they're both my daughters. They were born in a slightly unusual way, though."

I explained that they were slime spirits. I also wanted to head off the rumor that I had a husband before it got started.

I walked through the village, introducing my daughters to everyone.

"My, my! What adorable children."

"Are they ten or so?"

Actually, they were probably about fifty, but that would probably confuse everyone further.

Still, keeping quiet about it wouldn't have been good, either, so I explained.

At first, people looked startled, but they seemed to convince themselves. "If the great Witch is three hundred, it isn't too strange for her children to be fifty."

Since I'd walked Falfa and Shalsha through the village, they were now familiar faces. The villagers were already calling their names and greeting them.

Although the majority had trouble telling them apart.

The one with blue hair is the older sister, Falfa, and the one with light-green hair is the younger, Shalsha.

Incidentally, as I introduced the two of them to the villagers, I also did the reverse.

I was teaching my daughters about town. Since we were going to be living together, this would be our family's home territory.

"That's the bakery. Next to it is the clothing shop. They deal in secondhand clothing, too. Remember them so you don't get lost when you run errands."

"Okay, Mommy! I've already memorized them really good!"

"All right then, how many of the shops on the main road can you name?"

"Starting from the village's southern gate, there's Noelis the shoemaker and then the Meitz Dairy Products shop on the sixth block. On the fifth block, there's an abandoned building that was a general store until it closed down eight years ago, then the Kant Trading Company, which sells vegetable seeds and farming tools. The shop owner strained his back the other day."

"You know way too much!"

*So the shop that sells cheese and milk and things is called Meitz Dairy Products, hmm?* In three hundred years, I'd never bothered to notice its official name. I think the villagers would probably have gotten confused if someone had asked them where Meitz Dairy Products was, too.

"Did you memorize them, Shalsha?"

"...Uh-huh."

Shalsha seemed to be generally reserved, and I could still sense a little distance between us.

She had come to attack me, and as we'd done nothing as parent and child before this, in a way, it was inevitable.

*I guess we can just warm up to each other as time goes by.*

I was also a total beginner when it came to motherhood. It would have been stranger if I'd suddenly managed to be perfect at it.

"In that case, Shalsha, could you tell me how much you've learned about the village, too?"

"That slightly wider road is an old highway, and so if you look carefully, you can see traces of its past as a state road. Over there are the ruins of an Old Kingdom period checkpoint."

"I didn't tell you a single thing about any of that."

*What is she, a travel-show host?*

At any rate, I'd learned the two of them were extremely bright.

Spirits are special beings, aren't they? After fifty years, I guess you aren't just simple and innocent anymore.

"They certainly are your daughters, Lady Azusa. They're both clever."

Laika complimented them, but I thought they were long past "clever."

Just then, I heard a grumbly sound.

It was Laika's stomach.

"I-I'm sorry... I've walked more than usual today, so..."

Flustered, Laika blushed.

Were dragons well-behaved as a rule, or was this just Laika's personality? Maybe it was both.

"All right, well, that's the end of the tour. Why don't we go eat now?"

"Yaaay!"

"I'd like that."

It was good to see them so excited at the prospect, just like ordinary kids.

After that, the four of us ate together at the Savvy Eagle.

"Mommy, do I have to eat the celery, too?"

"Mom, I don't really like celery..."

Their attitudes relieved me a bit. *Oh, now they sound like actual children.*

"Well, if you eat it, you can order the chiffon cake afterward."

They seemed torn but took the plunge and scarfed down the celery.

"Very good. You mustn't be picky eaters."

One soup plate, however still retained its celery.

It was Laika's.

"You see, in my tribe, there is a rule that we must not eat it. We can eat other medicinal herbs, even if they're bitter, but..."

"Laika, if it's true, I don't mind, but don't lie to your teacher, all right?"

I pressed her gently.

"I-I'm terribly sorry! I'll eat it!"

So it had been a lie.

Laika squeezed her eyes shut and put the celery in her mouth.

"Oh, you're so gooood!"

Falfa patted Laika in the space between her horns.

It was like I'd picked up a third daughter.

I giggled in spite of myself.

I'd always enjoyed eating out, but this might have been the most fun I'd had yet.

At the very least, it was four times as much fun as being alone.

"I wonder why celery tastes like this...?"

Laika had "ugh" written all over her face, so I finished the rest of it for her.

I'd lived my laid-back life of solitude for three hundred years, but lately, there had been a sudden uptick in activity.

The reason was simple: I was now part of a family of four.

Actually, you don't have much opportunity for conversation when you live alone, so you almost never speak, you know?

Before I was reincarnated, on bad days, it wasn't unusual for the only conversation I had to be with the clerk at the neighborhood convenience store.

> Clerk: "That'll be one hundred eighty-three yen."
> Me: "Oh, I have exact change. Here you go: one hundred eighty-three yen."
> Clerk: "Here's your receipt. Thank you for your business."
> Me: "Mm-hmm."

…Like that.

This concludes my recollection of my past as a Japanese company peon.

I had many days like that, and I suspect that for lots of people, such conversations are the only ones they have.

In contrast, when there are four people in your family, you do a lot of talking.

For one thing, even when you're just greeting people, you have to go through three.

On a particular occasion, I was sophisticatedly perusing a grimoire I'd bought the other day. I'd gotten my turns for shopping and cooking out of the way the day before, so it was all right for me to take a load off. Incidentally, Laika was in charge of lunch.

"Here, Shalsha, look! I found it in the field!"

"You find those a lot, don't you, Sister?"

In the background, I heard the voices of my daughters at play.

It was safe to say I was spiritually content.

"This one goes really far!"

"Oh, you're right. That's a good flight distance."

*...What on earth are they talking about?*

Flight distance? Are they playing with a paper airplane or something? But this world has no concept of airplanes, does it...? What would it be, a paper dragon?

A grasshopper flew right in front of my book.

So *that* was what *flight distance* meant!

"Hey! Don't catch grasshoppers and bring them into the house!"

"Okaaaaay!"

"All right, Mom."

True, this area is a grassy plain, so there are lots of grasshoppers.

Still, I wish they wouldn't bring them inside.

When they started jumping around, it was pretty hard to catch them and take them out again.

"Then what should we catch?"

"I would prefer rabbits."

"Bunnies, huh? Last time, when I reached out with my tentacles, they nibbled on them."

Come to think of it, I hadn't seen my daughters extending their tentacles very often.

Slime spirits are able to do that. Actually, the appendages may look like hair, but strictly speaking, from what I hear, they're tentacles. Since there's no need for haircuts, it's nice and economical.

My two daughters were terribly intelligent spirits, but they played like children.

Maybe they were children at heart, or maybe their appearances influenced their actions.

*Since I've got the opportunity, let's listen in on my daughters' conversation.*

"Sister, would you like to read a book?"

"Uh-huh. I like the books you read to me, Shalsha. They're so interesting!"

"In that case, I'll read 'Clar Dynasty Commercial Policies in the Province of Hrant,' which is Section Two of Chapter Five in Volume Three of Lauretta's *History of the Rise and Fall of the Elvish People*."

*Talk about technical!*

And that wasn't even the right genre for reading to somebody else.

I hadn't had a thick book like that one in the house, so it most likely belonged to Shalsha.

*She really does like history, doesn't she...?*

"Heranke, the founder of the Clar Dynasty, was originally a merchant who amassed his fortune trading in dried fruit. Before long, his private army grew into a mighty force equal to the military powers among the elves of the Hrant province. Eventually, in the year 405, he proclaimed himself king. As a result, the Clar Dynasty treated dried fruit as the most important export for acquiring foreign capital, but—"

And she was actually reading that specialized text ...

By the way, she mentioned the word *elves*—naturally, they exist in this world.

At present, the elves don't have a large country of their own. They're based in forested areas all over, and several groups resemble small countries and are recognized as self-governing.

The Clar Dynasty Shalsha had spoken of was probably one of these small nations.

Elves were known for being long-lived, and they sometimes made friends with immortal witches. I'd never left my highlands, though, so I didn't have any elf acquaintances.

It wasn't that there were no forests here, but they probably weren't large enough for elves to build villages and towns and live there.

*Bam-bam, bam-bam.*

Someone was knocking on the door.

*Who could that be?* My daughters were right in front of me, and Laika was in the kitchen, making soup with beans we'd just harvested.

"Mom... Do you want me to get that?"

"I appreciate the offer, but no thank you."

Worst-case scenario, it could have been somebody who'd come to attack me.

The tale of the strongest witch might have been spreading like wildfire. I couldn't make my daughters go.

Cautiously, I opened the door.

"Yes? Who is it?"

A young elf woman was standing there with tears in her eyes.

All else aside, her figure was bizarrely good.

An ample bosom and a generous derriere.

Not only that, but that was one short skirt. She was an extraordinarily voluptuous elf.

She was sexy enough that, if my children had been boys, I would have wanted to keep her out of sight for the sake of their upbringing.

To be honest, I rather wish she'd share a little of that bust with me. Just once, I'd like to complain that my chest is so heavy that my shoulders get stiff.

Well, never mind that.

"Um, what did you need?"

I hadn't expected an elf to show up immediately after I'd heard my daughter mention them, but this sort of coincidence is actually fairly common. For example, you read a book on Kamakura, and Kamakura turns up on a travel program on TV the same day. Things like that.

"I... I want you to save me!"

She extended her hands in front of her as she spoke, and her breasts were trapped between her arms.

Thanks to that, her bust looked even bigger. Was she trying to suggest something?

Apparently, the girl in question hadn't emphasized her bust on purpose. She wasn't being suggestive.

I was a woman, so there was no sense in using sex appeal on me. She was just being herself.

"You want me to save you? There aren't any orcs around here."

When elves or female knights are being targeted by something, it's always orcs, isn't it?

"Not from orcs! I want you to save me from that high-ranking demon Beelzebub!"

Now that was a disturbing name.

Beelzebub.

An incredibly high-level demon, also known as the Lord of the Flies.

In a game, the type that would probably come right before the final boss.

Frankly, I didn't want to fight that.

*P-tunk.*

I slowly closed the door.

The elf opened it again right away.

"I'm begging you! The Witch of the Highlands was the only person I could think of who might help me!"

"I don't want to fight a scary monster, either!"

FYI, in this world, the far north of the continent was so cold that almost nothing could live there.

In the depths of that place, the more intelligent monsters (known as demons) had created a country of sorts—or so I'd heard.

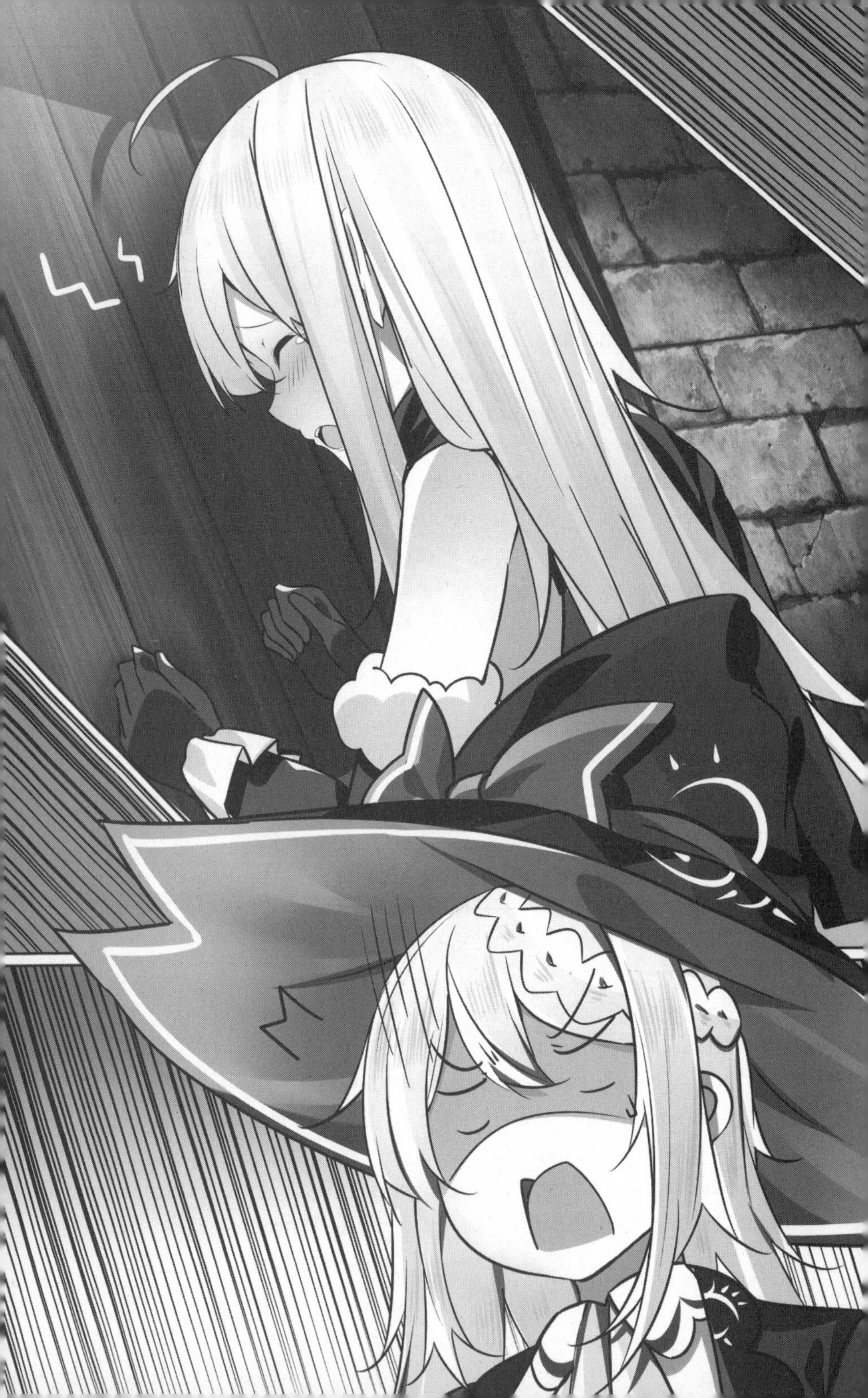

It was too cold for ordinary people to reach it, so nobody really knew.

In the past, they had ostensibly fought with the human nations, but things had been peaceful for the last five hundred years.

Which was why, unless we picked a fight with them, things were bound to stay peaceful going forward, too.

However, I had the feeling that if I made contact with this Beelzebub character, my peace would be threatened...

"Please! At least hear me out! When I asked the people of my village, they said they didn't want to get dragged into this and told me to get out, and now I have nowhere to go... I thought that since the Witch of the Highlands was renowned as the most powerful, she might be able to do something..."

"If I hear you out, will you go home?"

"P-please save me! If Beelzebub comes after me, I'm sure to be killed..."

*If she's going to go that far, I guess I can't just chase her away.*

*I suppose I'll do what I can to help.*

*Only "what I can," though.*

All-out war with a monster nation would destroy our quartet's way of life, so I wanted nothing to do with it.

"Well, tell me your story. Yes, come in."

When they saw the young visitor, Falfa and Shalsha commented:

"It's an elf!"

"Her ears are indeed long. By the way, if her earwax is dry, she's a southern elf, while the earwax of northern elves is wet."

The two of them entered the room together.

Shalsha seemed to know a lot about elves and geography, so I thought it best to let them stay for this.

"All right, let's start by introducing ourselves. You already know people call me the Witch of the Highlands, so I'll just tell you my name. I'm the witch Azusa Aizawa."

"I'm Halkara. I'm from a small elf country in the province of Hrant."

That region had just come up in the history book Shalsha was reading.

"There are all sorts of medicinal herbs in the area, and I've taken advantage of that to become an apothecary... In short, my job is very much like yours, Madam Witch."

We're both long-lived, we both make medicines out of plants... We really are similar.

In this case, there's no real difference between the "witch" and "apothecary" classes.

Truth be told, it wouldn't be fair to call myself an apothecary.

If I had to differentiate us, witches sometimes use materials from animals, such as dried organs and blood. An elf apothecary probably stuck exclusively to plants and didn't even include special ores or other minerals.

I didn't use many animal materials, though, so I was pretty close to being an apothecary anyway.

Just then, Laika brought in enough herbal tea for all of us. Tea for four, including portions for my two daughters. This when she'd been busy cooking. *Thank you for the trouble.*

"I understand about your profession, but why is Beelzebub hunting an apothecary?"

I couldn't think of any reason they'd even have met each other.

"Well, I feel a little awkward saying this myself, but for an apothecary, I made a very good living. I combined nutrient-rich mushrooms and botanicals and turned them into a liquor known as Nutri-Spirits."

*So alcohol with herbal medicine mixed in?*

"If you drink it when you're tired, you can endure the rest of your work. It took the whole region by storm and became a huge hit. All the elves in my village worked together to mass-produce bottles that sold for five thousand gold each, and even then, production couldn't keep up. I actually built a Nutri-Spirits palace in my village."

*All right, enough bragging. Get on with the story.*

"Oh, and this is it."

Halkara produced a small bottle.

"I brought a lot with me, so you can drink it if you'd like. It was hard to carry so much while I was running away, but when I drank it, it got me through the day."

By all accounts (and appearances), this was an energy drink, wasn't it?

I used to drink these things regularly, once upon a time. Her tale hit painfully close to home.

When my overtime dragged on, I'd down a bottle...

"Its reputation generated more popularity, and Nutri-Spirits came to be sold far away. And so, you see, it ended up with some unexpected customers..."

Halkara held her head in her hands.

"From what I'm told, a person named Beelzebub, who was a high-ranking demon—so by *person*, I suppose I mean *demon*—got ahold of some and drank it."

"What happened?"

"In humans and elves, it energizes them and fills them with strength, but for demons, it's apparently toxic... Ten minutes after ingesting it, Beelzebub collapsed, developed a high fever, and came dangerously close to going to hell."

It didn't seem as though going to hell would be a problem for a high-ranking demon, but I guess I was wrong.

"In other words, Beelzebub has been revived and is after you now."

"Yes! From what I hear, that demon is furious, swearing up and down that the person who made this deadly poison will pay with their life. A wanted poster written in the demon tongue has been distributed even in areas inhabited by humans and elves."

She held out a piece of paper, but I haven't studied Demon, so I couldn't read it.

"I know a little bit."

Shalsha peeked in.

"Please...find...woman make...Nutri-Spirits liquor...generous... reward...offered— If you just read each word by itself, that's more or less what it says."

That's Shalsha for you. Her knowledge really is extensive.

The words suggested it was indeed a genuine wanted poster.

"All my employees got scared and fled. On top of that, I've been banned from the village... And that's why I came to you, Madam Witch. I beg you! Please save me!"

Halkara rose from her chair, prostrating herself before me.

"It's clear you're in trouble, but...if we aren't careful, couldn't this turn into total war with the demons?"

No matter how you sliced it, I couldn't handle that.

"Um, you see...the elves and the province where my village is have identified that risk, so they decided it might be better to hand the 'elf apothecary' over to the demons. I have nowhere to go!"

Not only did she have no home to return to, she was being treated as a criminal...

It was hard not to have some compassion.

"Poor elf lady..."

"You don't have a home... It's hard just looking at you..."

My daughters both expressed their sympathy.

I couldn't just tell her to leave now. It would set a bad example for my daughters.

*But no way I'm fighting Beelzebub for this girl.*

I couldn't put my daughters and Laika in danger. It didn't matter how strong I was—even if I could hold my own against individuals, there are limits to how effectively one person could fight organizations or countries.

We'd have to hit on a good compromise.

I sighed.

"All right. I'll help you."

"Thank you so much!"

Halkara flung herself at me and hugged me. She's a bit generous with physical contact...

"That said, I don't plan to confront Beelzebub, either. I'll hide you here, at my house. Let's wait and watch until the storm blows over."

As long as people didn't know she was with me, it was bound to work itself out.

"Does that mean I won't be able to leave this building?"

"No, I don't think we'll need to go to that extreme. We'll be in trouble if people find out, though, so let's give you a disguise and an alias."

Fortunately, her occupation was similar to mine.

Not only that, but since she was a long-lived elf, she wouldn't be out of place at a witch's house.

I went to my room and brought back a robe I didn't usually wear.

"Wear this when you go out. You're the second apprentice of Azusa, 'the Witch of the Highlands.'"

And so I turned my visitor into a false apprentice.

The robe had fit me…

"I'm sorry. It seems a bit snug."

…but the fabric was stretched tight over her bust and her rear, and it looked rather wanton.

*We'll have to go to the village and have something tailored…*

The next day, I woke up fairly early in the morning.

The first thing I did was cast a barrier over my house in the highlands.

The fact that Halkara had managed to flee all the way here meant there was a good chance she hadn't been followed, but I shored up our defenses just in case.

"Ye with wicked hearts, may this net ensnare you and rob you of freedom. As if by its own will, it shall fall on thee… HAAAAAaaaaaah! —Right. That came out nicely."

This barrier had been quite a bit easier than the one I'd cast over the village. After all, it was on a totally different scale.

After that, I made sandwiches for the whole family's lunch.

It was my turn to take care of the meals. Oh, and for breakfast, I recycled—er, "adapted"—leftovers from what Laika had made the day before.

According to our system, it was okay to use food from the previous day. However, you did need to make something new. For that reason, while I prepared sandwiches, I was also making a soup with mixed grains and medicinal herbs.

It was good for you and also helped keep your face from swelling.

My daughters had initially balked at the unique taste of the herbs, but they'd grown used to it.

Some people aren't fond of coriander at first, but they gradually develop a marked preference for it. Lots of medicinal herbs are that way. They have robust flavors, but you can develop an equally robust appreciation for them.

As an aside, even if you're a spirit or immortal, you start feeling sick when you eat badly, so it's important to take care of your health.

All right. Why was I making lunch in the morning? Because I was going out.

My purpose was to gather medicinal herbs. That was something I did for work, but this day was a bit special.

It just so happened I had an elf who knew a lot about curative flora, so I thought I'd have her make medicine with me.

Besides, it would seem unnatural if I had no idea what sort of curatives my apprentice made.

Laika woke up before long, and Shalsha and Falfa came in after her, rubbing their eyes. Apparently, Shalsha always woke first and then roused her older sister, Falfa.

"Good morning..."

Halkara was the last one up.

I'd just about finished fixing the meal at that point.

Everyone, including me, called, "Morning!" "Good morning."

"I hadn't slept in a proper bed in so long… I was really happy. Thank you."

"Yes, yes, well, everyone needs a little help sometimes. Don't worry about it. Oh, that's right. Starting today, you'll need to act as my apprentice in earnest. I'll be more familiar with you, so be ready for that."

"Oh yes, please, go ahead. Address me casually or any way you like, Madam Teacher!"

"Madam Teacher…? That's not wrong, so I suppose it's okay."

Then Halkara sat down, too, and we ate breakfast.

After a little while, for some reason, Halkara began quietly sobbing.

"Um, is something the matter…?"

"I ate out constantly when I was busy with work, and when I was on the run, I gathered nuts and berries in the forest to ward off starvation some days… It's been so long since I sat at a warm, friendly table like this one."

As she cried, Halkara's shoulders rounded forward, giving her the hunched back of someone who'd been through a lot.

I'd seen people like this in Japan, too.

Individuals who'd succeeded in business before being ruined and falling on hard times.

In Halkara's case, her business hadn't exactly failed, but her life was definitely headed downhill.

*Somebody has to extend a helping hand. If no one does, she's going to die.*

*I'll help as much as I can.*

"Halkara, cheer up."

Falfa went around behind Halkara's chair and began thumping her shoulders lightly to give her a massage. What a good girl.

"Oh… Falfa, wasn't it? Thank you very much," Halkara said.

"If I'd known this was going to happen, I would never have expanded my business… If I'd kept things modest and sold medicine only in my own province…"

She'd expanded her business, and it had backfired. This really did seem like a case of corporate failure.

"Yes, all right, there's no sense in brooding. Let's think about what to do next."

I clapped my hands briskly.

"Once we're finished eating, we'll go gather herbs in the forest near here. Show me what you can do, Halkara. The rest of you, stay here and keep an eye on the house."

"Y-yes, Madam Teacher!"

"By the way, I've made sandwiches for lunch, so you and the others eat those, Laika."

"All right, Lady Azusa. We'll do some investigating with regards to Beelzebub on our end."

"Yes, please do."

It was prudent to be as prepared as possible.

"Also, I'm sure it's probably still all right, but if the enemy does come, please take care of Falfa and Shalsha."

"I will, even if it costs me my life!"

"No, protect your own life, too, Laika. If anything happens, just tell them where I am."

Demons were extremely intelligent, high-level monsters, and in the three hundred years I'd lived in this world, I'd never heard of them committing atrocities against humans. That was why I doubted they'd attack indiscriminately. Still, having a solid defense was most definitely a good thing.

"Although I can't advise being too optimistic, it doesn't sound as though anyone connected with Halkara has been attacked, so there's a good possibility they won't target your daughters."

"Yes, I hope you're right about that."

We'd done all we could for the moment, so Halkara and I set off for the forest.

Just in case you were wondering, the elf's clothes were still stretched very tightly.

"Listen, Halkara… Do people ever tell you you're well-developed?"

Being too straightforward could have been considered sexual harassment, so I used a more neutral expression.

I'd determined to ask the question early on precisely because it was rather touchy.

"I'm told I have a lascivious body about seven hundred fifty times a year."

"That's twice a day!"

"The elves in the province where I used to live tend to be slender, so I stood out far too much. I'm completely used to it now, though, so you don't need to be careful around me."

"I see…"

"It irritated me that all people saw was my body. That was why I worked hard to make it as an apothecary. I did eventually start selling a lot of medicine, but it got me nowhere seeing as how Beelzebub is after me… Ha-ha-ha…"

Life just doesn't go the way you want it to, does it?

In the course of that conversation, we reached the woods.

Immediately, we bent down and began gathering plants.

The things we scavenged went into our baskets, which were conveniently designed to be carried on our backs.

My priority during this outing was watching how Halkara worked.

It didn't matter if I didn't gather much. Frankly, my harvest was just a bonus.

If she was using plants I didn't, I wanted her to teach me about them.

I hadn't spent much time with anyone else in my profession, and an information exchange would have been welcome.

Halkara's gaze seemed more focused on the trees and ground than on the grasses.

"Ah-ha, there you are, there you are."

She plucked a mushroom clinging to a tree root.

Then she picked another one from the ground.

And another she found hiding quietly in the thick grass.

And a scary one that was brightly colored and probably poisonous.

"You're only picking mushrooms!"

I sometimes use these, too, of course, but I'm never this thorough about harvesting them. In fact, some of Halkara's selections were ones I'd always ignored.

"Mushrooms are my field of expertise. Only in medicine, though. Some of these are poisonous and dangerous if ingested raw."

"True, toxic ingredients can be used as medicine sometimes."

"Maybe it's because of the different climate in my hometown, but the variety here is quite unusual. These are definitely worth gathering!"

Halkara continued to focus on mushrooms—or rather, exclusively mushrooms.

She seemed more like a mycologist than an apothecary.

"This is a Great Dawn King Mushroom. This one is a Great Circle Mushroom. There's a Tumbling Mouse Mushroom, too."

I knew all the names, but there were quite a few I didn't remember ever using as medicine.

Come to think of it, the concoctions witches make have something like regional characteristics.

Since plants vary by area, this is unsurprising, but even so…

Although they weren't the least bit dangerous to me, monsters did haunt these woods.

Whenever one seemed liable to attack Halkara, I eliminated it and collected its magic stone.

At some point, Halkara's Mushroom Lecture Time began. I'd be able to use the information for future reference, so I listened carefully.

"This mushroom is poisonous."

"Yes, I know. The red is obviously too deep, and it just looks shady."

"Actually, if you boil it for about ten minutes, the poison breaks down! After that, it's delicious, and you can use it in meals!"

"Huh?! You can?"

"By the way, when connoisseurs eat it, they tend to intentionally leave a little of the poison. Apparently, it makes them warm, and the effect is very pleasant."

Yes, because reckless daredevils can be found anywhere.

"This Roly-Poly Mushroom is small, so almost no one pays any attention to it. However, it has an interesting texture when eaten, and if you add it to sautés, it serves as a nice accent."

"Wait, you can eat that one, too? They don't even eat this kind in the villages around here."

"It won't fill your belly, and they may not generally offer it for sale."

Learning all manner of things from the mushroom mage, before I knew it, it was time for lunch.

It's true that, when you have a specialist around, even the mundane turns out to be filled with all sorts of things you didn't know.

The world looks different through the eyes of a professional. This was tremendously informative.

I also picked up several more recipes for mushroom dishes. I'd make them for Laika and my daughters one of these days.

"I had no idea this herb-gathering trip would turn out to be so inspiring. Thank you!"

I'd really had more to gain than I'd imagined. All hail Queen Halkara.

"No, no, I'm thrilled you enjoyed yourself. I'm not familiar with a lot of the plants here. Please teach me about them next time, Madam Teacher."

It was true. Simply by virtue of being a local, I did seem to know more about them than Halkara did.

Just because she was an elf didn't mean her knowledge of medicines was perfect in every respect.

When it came to plants that weren't native to your area, your knowledge was bound to be limited.

"Plus, when monsters attacked, you got rid of them for me, Madam Teacher! The rumors of your tremendous strength were true!"

"Just leave the monsters in this forest to me."

After all, I'm not level 99 for nothing.

I'd never lose to the low-level monsters you run into in these woods.

I've only ever killed slimes and giant monster rabbits, but just encountering the latter had been enough to make Halkara lose her cool.

"Well, shall we have lunch? I brought sandwiches."

They were the ones I'd risen early to make.

"I'd love to, thank you! But you've done so much for me already, Madam Teacher. Let me cook something, too, please!"

With that, Halkara took out a mesh grill and an item we would have called a spirit lamp in Japan.

It reminded me of a cooking experiment I'd done a very long time ago.

She set her tools up on a flat rock. So it was like a simple barbecue...

"On days when I gather mushrooms, I like to cook the edible ones on a screen this way and eat them! There's a brook over there, so I'll be able to rinse the dirt off our ingredients. We're in the perfect spot for this!"

"Mushrooms, hmm? That does sound delicious, but make sure not to include any poisonous ones."

Halkara thumped her chest.

"Have no fear! My knowledge of fungi is infallible!"

I guess I'll trust the expert.

As we waited for the mushrooms to grill, we ate the sandwiches I'd made.

"Ah, the little ones are done!"

Halkara produced a bottle containing a black liquid.

"This is a sauce known as 'elvin.' It's an essential part of the elf diet, so much so that it takes its name from the word *elf*."

She drizzled some over a roasted mushroom.

It sizzled, and the sound really did whet the appetite.

The moisture had been nicely grilled out of the mushrooms, and in some, it had pooled in the caps to become a kind of soup.

*Huh? This aroma reminds me a little of soy sauce!*

"Elvin is made by fermenting several types of beans. I think the flavor would be well received nationwide, but they don't make too much of it."

*So it is a cousin of soy sauce!*

I impaled a steaming mushroom with a fork.

It was hot, so I blew on it, put it into my mouth, and—

"Ooooooh! It's delicious!"

*Simple is best! This is fantastic!*

The elvin did taste similar to soy sauce.

It was more pungent, but that was probably due to the fermentation method.

"Oh man, sake! If I had sake, this would be perfect!"

I was inspired to blurt out things like *Why don't we have any beer?!* By the way, this world does have an alcoholic drink that's a lot like beer.

"Go on, eat up, please! Every kind has a different texture!"

Who'd have thought we'd have a mushroom party in the woods?

Each species had its own unique characteristics, and they never got boring.

If I kept this up, I could probably become a mushroom sommelier.

"There are still all kinds of edible ones left. This next one is a Flower-Cap Rainbow Mushroom."

Halkara kept grilling her assortment of fungi.

They also varied widely in hue, so much so that I marveled that the forest had been so colorful.

"Still, I've been blind. I didn't know so many edible mushrooms existed. The forest is a treasure trove of ingredients, isn't it?"

"It certainly is. Elves aren't forest dwellers for nothing. You can use these in medicine and eat them, toooo! Heh-heh-heh-heh!"

Halkara's spirits were soaring.

True, eating outdoors around a fire this way lent our meal a festive atmosphere.

"I, Halkara, would like to teach the villagers how to make the best possible use of the forest's bounty, so please assist me in that as well! Heh-heh-heh-heh!"

"That's a great idea! They'll be thrilled!"

We didn't have anything alcoholic, so we struck our canteens against each other in a makeshift toast.

"I'll need to let my daughters and Laika try this, too. I have to tell them about what mushrooms can do."

"Yes, with my knowledge, I can teach you as much as you like in that regard! Heh-heh-heh-heh-heh-heh-heh-heh!"

"Halkara, come on, you're laughing too much."

"You're riiight. I think I'm laughing too much, toooo. I just can't seem to stooop. Heh-heh-heh-heh-heh!"

*Huh?*

*What does she mean, she can't stop...?*

"Um, Halkara... Are you sure you haven't eaten a poisonous mushroom?"

"I'm a mushroom expert. I doooo know about mushrooms. Thiiiis is a Brown Shadow Mushroom, you see? And thiiiis is a Crimson Maiden Mushroom. Thiiiis is a poisonous Cow's Smile Mushroom."

"So one of those *was* poisonous!"

"Huh......?"

For a few moments, Halkara went still.

"Oops. I see, I see. I may have the knowledge, but I was careless when I sorted them and accidentally put a poisonous one in with the edible oooones. Heh! Heh-heh-heh-heh-heh-heh!"

"You know your stuff, but you're not using it!"

Carelessness overrules expertise!

"Hey, is it okay for you to eat poison? Shouldn't you, um, bring it back up?"

"Oh, this one's not a problem. It just makes you laaaaugh. I'll be laughing for an hour or so, that's aaaall. Heh-heh-heh-heh!"

She wasn't cackling. She was just chuckling in a closed-mouthed sort of way, almost like she was smiling. It was actually pretty creepy. Well, it was a "cow's smile" mushroom, after all.

"If I haven't developed symptoms, it must mean I haven't eaten one, right? Yes, I hadn't touched that one yet."

"True. *Pfft!*"

*That laugh sounds kinda pretentious.*

"Listen, I'm worried now. Would you check the other mushrooms, too? You set a variety aside as 'edible.'"

"All right, I'll double-check all of them. Stripy Wave Mushrooms aren't poisonous. Tapered Orange Mushrooms aren't. Triangular Chestnut Mushrooms are."

"There was another poisonous type in there!"

"Aaaaaaaah! You're right! I put one from the medicinal zone in!"

*Should someone this absentminded be making medicine…?*

I could just see her casually admitting, *Whoops, sorry, that was a lethal dose.*

"I hadn't eaten that kind yet, either. Guess that's a small mercy."

"I did."

*She lives like she's a walking biomedical experiment.*

Even when it didn't come through in her voice, Halkara kept smiling due to the effect of the poison.

"What sort of symptoms does this one give you?"

"It causes pleasant mental and physical elation, but unlike a drug, it isn't habit-forming. Sometimes I powder it and mix some into a prescription for terribly depressed people. If taken in large amounts, it's said to have an aphrodisiac effect."

"An aphro—what?"

I had heard her correctly but really hoped I hadn't.

"It means it temporarily makes you feel like being naughty— Huh?"

Halkara began steadily gazing at me.

She took a step forward.

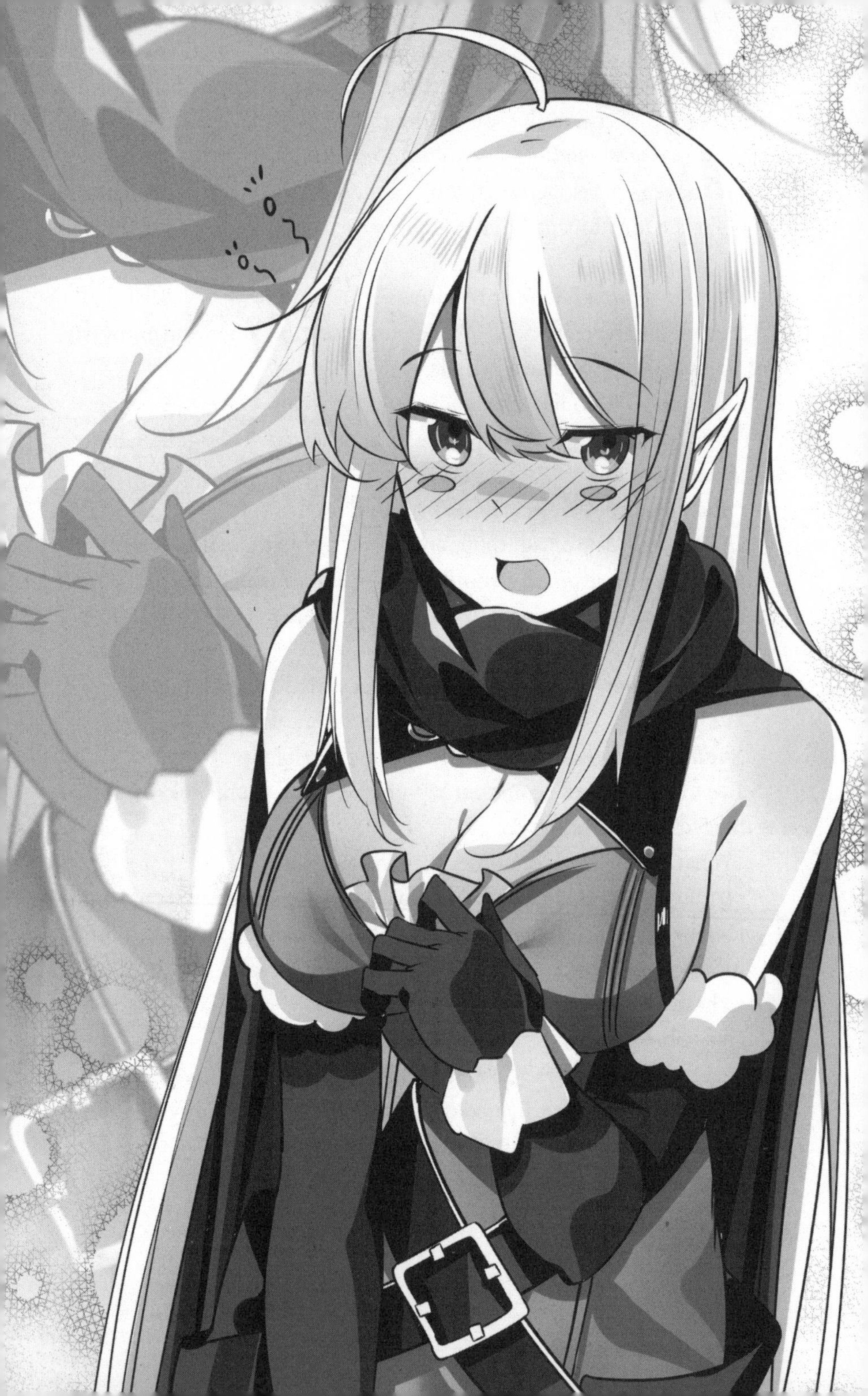

I was getting nervous, so I took a step back.

"Why are you backing away, Madam Teacher?"

"Because you might have been poisoned."

Halkara slid her fingers into her neckline in a way that emphasized her cleavage.

"Madam Teacher, w-would you like to do something fun with me...? Actually, please do."

"No thanks!"

That toxin had definitely kicked in.

I took to my heels. Danger was approaching!

Naturally, Halkara followed.

"It's all right! I promise it'll feel really good!"

"That's not what I base my decisions on!"

Good thing I hadn't brought Falfa and Shalsha along...

This would have been inappropriate, and it would have been no laughing matter if she tried to make a move on my daughters.

Technically, I did have the Levitation spell, so if all I was doing was running away, I could have won easily. However, leaving a wanton elf with her figure on the loose in the woods was probably unwise.

You could say that, as her teacher, her well-being was my responsibility, and if she ran into a villager hunting for animals, Halkara's virtue would come into question.

"Wait! I have a Detoxify spell, don't I?!"

I thrust my right hand out at Halkara.

Only...Detox isn't effective unless you touch the other person...

The mere act of touching Halkara seemed risky. I suspected she'd try something on me before I detoxified her completely.

*I—I think I'll just keep running...!*

"Please wait, Madam Teacher!"

"In a way, my apprentice, you're lucky I'm a woman."

I couldn't deny that, had I been male, I could have succumbed to my desires.

Halkara's body just seemed that incredibly soft. It curved in all the right places.

Conversely, her body type didn't give her an athletic advantage, so I led Halkara along steadily, frequently glancing back to check on her.

Why was I doing that? Because this was a forest, and it had its dangers.

Abruptly, Halkara's face disappeared from view.

"Agh! I'm falling, I'm gonna faaaaall!"

Halkara had taken a misstep and was beginning to slip down a slope.

It was dirt, so she probably wouldn't die, but it was likely she'd sprain a leg or get scraped up.

"Oh, honestly…!"

I quickly turned back, stretched out a hand, and grabbed one of Halkara's.

Agility: 841.

My staggering stats had made this possible.

"Y-you've saved my life…Madam Teacher…"

"You're a troublesome apprentice, aren't you?"

"You saved me. Does that mean you really do like me, Madam Teacher?"

"It still hasn't worn off…"

Later, once all the poison was out of her system, Halkara kept bowing and bowing and bowing in apology.

"I'm terribly sorry! Really! I'm sorry! I caused you so much trouble!"

"You sure did. Still, what's done is done, and there's no point in talking about it. Let's consider it water under the bridge."

"Thank you so much!"

Halkara smiled.

This apothecary made a lot of mistakes, but it was hard to hate that smile.

"If you seem likely to cause trouble again, though, I'll make that call."

"Call? Call what?"

"Beelzebub."

Halkara went pale. "Anything but that!"

That afternoon, after Halkara and I returned from the forest, we began brewing pharmaceuticals.

That hadn't been part of the plan, but Halkara had remarked, "I'd like to sell medicine to earn money."

Apothecaries did everything from manufacturing medicine to selling it, and apparently, she wanted to earn money on her own to contribute to the house's income. "I'm lodging with you for nothing, so I can't act high and mighty," she explained.

Everything one needed to make medicine was already in place.

Since a witch—yours truly—had lived in this house for so many long years, it had a lab.

There was also a small room for drying herbs and mushrooms.

This was because some types became less effective if they contained moisture.

When it came to mixing medicines, Halkara did things properly.

However, rather than curing diseases or treating symptoms, most of her concoctions were meant to maintain health or give the body energy. They were the type you were supposed to take daily.

"With natural remedies, I think it's all right to compound them this way."

"I know, but do they work on illness?"

"It's more efficient to make the body itself healthy, isn't it?"

If my values were closer to those of Western medicine, Halkara's were probably nearer to traditional Eastern medicine.

It wasn't a question of which was better. Both were necessary.

For that reason, I was grateful she had come here. There was a lot I could gain from this as well.

Of course, I'd also made elixirs with the villagers' health in mind, but I hadn't devoted any real thought to giving them something to take on a regular basis.

Besides, daily pills got expensive, so they were hard to sell.

Apparently, since Halkara could make hers with relative ease, she was able to keep her prices down.

Around then, Laika brought in some herbal tea. "You two must be tired from all your hard work."

"Thank you, Laika. Were the girls good?"

"After we had lunch, they got sleepy and went down for a nap right away. They might have risen earlier than usual this morning. They're asleep on the same bed."

"It's tempting to go peek at them while they're sleeping, but I might wake them, so I'll refrain."

Those two really were incredibly cute when they were asleep. Especially when they'd gotten tired and started napping on the same bed. They were so adorable that it was frustrating that this world had no cameras.

"How did your herb gathering go?"

Halkara's face went red.

"I messed up..."

"Messed up?"

"I'm sorry. Please don't ask for details. I'm so embarrassed I could die..."

I thought it would be mean to kick her when she was down, so I decided to keep quiet.

"Well then, Halkara. Tomorrow, if the weather's nice, I'll introduce you to the village. It's a small place, so word will travel quickly either way."

"All right. I leave it to you, Madam Teacher!"

Halkara went out of her way to raise a hand as she responded.

Everything about her was indiscreet.

She'd been running a company up until now, which made me

wonder how that had really gone for her, but actually, it was likely you couldn't do big things like that without a certain lack of discretion. After all, somebody cautious would never launch a business.

On the other hand, you could say the mushroom-sorting mix-up had been the result of that same recklessness.

It was both a good and bad thing. This was tricky stuff.

"Prepare some medicine to take along tomorrow, then. There's a shop that sells things for me on consignment. We'll say this is a curative the new witch made and leave it there."

"All right! In that case, it would be best if I made it something distinct from yours, Madam Teacher."

"True. Those pills that help your digestive system might be good—or the ones that restore missing nutrients."

Would these be called health supplements?

After that, I looked Halkara up and down again.

"We should also get some clothes tailored for you."

This outfit wasn't keeping Halkara's charms in check at all. It might have been a bit shy on fabric.

"Um, this is fine, though. It feels as though it's stretched out as I've been wearing it."

"Stretched out... It did, huh...?"

I wasn't very interested in her stats, but I was terribly curious about her measurements.

At dinner, we set the mushrooms Halkara had picked on the table.

I'd had her check to make absolutely sure none of them were poisonous before she cooked them.

Ingesting poison wasn't good for anybody, but the damage could have been particularly serious for my daughters' small bodies.

"If you slice these Stripy Wave Mushrooms, then sauté them with lean chicken, broccoli, and a lot of salt, they're pretty good. It goes well with liquor, too."

I had taken the opportunity to stand in the kitchen and watch her cook.

"Flower-Cap Rainbow Mushrooms get tough, so let's put them in a stew."

Was this mushroom-style improvised cooking?

Halkara's dishes went over incredibly well, and I was quite satisfied, too.

Thanks to her, the recipe repertoire of the house in the highlands looked poised to expand quite a bit.

The next day, the sky was clear, so Halkara and I set out for the village of Flatta together.

We encountered slimes along the way, so I hunted them down with precision, then picked up the magic stones.

"Madam Teacher, you really are adept at eliminating slimes, aren't you?"

"Yes, because I've been doing it for three centuries. I'm like the curator of a traditional craft technique. You try it this time, Halkara."

Halkara brandished a staff made of oak.

"Take that, and that!"

They bounced.

Her breasts bounced like you wouldn't believe.

It was so bad it made you want to ask, *Which one's the slime, huh?*

"Whew... I managed to kill one, somehow."

"Lucky..."

"What is?"

"No, it's nothing. Never mind."

There are probably lots of drawbacks like stiff shoulders and whatnot, but for just one day, I would love to experience that feeling for myself.

And so, earning spare change as we went, we reached Flatta.

The village was as peaceful as ever.

"The air in highland villages is delightful, isn't it? It's so dry, somehow."

"That's what I hear. I've never left the area, so I don't really know the difference."

*All right, we should probably take a casual walk around the village first.*

Since she was going to be living with me, it was better to introduce her to everyone early on and get it out of the way.

After all, if people thought she was a mystery elf, they'd gossip more. If I told them she was my apprentice, it would be easier to convince them.

That aside, my family had been growing fast lately.

If you live a long time, your family is probably bound to expand sometimes. I bet so.

I thought we'd begin by walking down the street lined with shops, which also happened to be the village's main road.

Whenever we saw people, we'd greet each and every one of them. "Good morning." "Good morning." I felt like a politician with an election coming up.

Of course, "Good morning" wasn't the goal. What I was doing was introducing Halkara.

First, I spotted an old woman passing by.

"Good morning!"

"Well, well, great Witch of the Highlands. Good morning to you."

In this village, there's no one who doesn't know the Witch of the Highlands.

I have an approval rating of 100 percent. Usually, that only happens in a dictatorship.

It's the result of the trust I've built up over three hundred years.

"I've come to introduce my new apprentice. This is my elf student, Akikana."

"I-I'm Akikana... I make medicines! I'll work very hard!"

"Oh, an elf, eh? Don't see many of those myself. It's good to meet you."

*Great, that's one down.*

If I kept this up for a good long time, "Akikana" was bound to blend into the village.

After that, no one would be thinking that some weird elf had joined their number.

Naturally, Akikana was an alias.

If we'd introduced her as Halkara, people who knew about the wanted poster might catch on.

However, partway through our self-introductions, the atmosphere turned noticeably strange.

About one in every two villagers reacted awkwardly.

I didn't really get why at first, but gradually, I started to understand.

Nearly every single man was looking at Halkara's chest.

At one point, there was a passerby who was like, "I-I've never seen a-a bosom like that in this village..." and a boy who was exclaimed, "Lady, your boobs are humongous!" so I doubted I was mistaken.

"Say, do men really pay that much attention to busts? You'd think one or two wouldn't care, right?"

Was this even possible at a rate of 100 percent? Usually, that only happens in a dictatorship. About one person in ten isn't really a fan of big boobs, right? This was on a whole different kind of notoriety.

"Oh... No, this is how it usually goes. I know they're looking at me. Having men notice me is embarrassing, but...it's sort of my lot in life, so..."

Halkara seemed to have given up. Having a sizable chest is rougher than you'd think.

"Even with people who say they prefer smaller breasts, their eyes just gravitate toward an ample bosom when they see it, or so I've heard. It's a little like being startled by someone very tall."

"I see."

"So, Madam Teacher, believe in yourself, please."

"Excuse me?! Don't talk like I don't believe in myself!"

"Even if your bust is small, you can live with confidence!"

"Don't call it 'small' outright like that! A-anyway, it's not that small!"

*What a rude apprentice.*

Next, we stopped by the village general store.

This was the shop that sold my medicines on consignment for me.

I was planning to have them stock Halkara's as well. They had no real reason to refuse, so the matter was settled easily.

"I'm Akikana, an elf apothecary. I look forward to doing business with you. These are pills I've made. This type is good for digestion, and the others may be used as a nutritional supplement."

The man who ran the shop said, "You betcha. If you're the great Witch of the Highlands' apprentice, they'll sell real well."

But then, for some reason, his expression clouded.

"Erm, young lady... You're an apothecary, you said? About how many years have you been doing that?"

"Oh, are you concerned about my ingredients since I said I've just become an apprentice?! I did become a student recently, but I've been working as an apothecary for several decades at least!"

"I-is that right...? In other words, you're an elf with a long career as an apothecary..."

What was this? This was starting to feel like an interrogation.

Was something suspicious about us?

"By the way, what province are you from?"

"Hrant."

"I see... No, don't worry about it. I bet it's some sort of mistake. I'm positive."

I really wanted to ask what exactly this was about, but suspecting it would come back to bite me, we just left the shop.

"All right, we've accomplished our main objective. Now we'll just go around greeting people and go home."

"You're right. Um, earlier, I felt like he was asking a lot of questions about my background… About where my province was and things…"

"Maybe your accent caught his attention. Different regions have different intonation, you know. Ha-ha…"

After that, while we made our round of introductions, people stared at Halkara an awful lot.

Up until a minute earlier, the only stares had been male and directed at her chest, but now we were getting them from the women as well.

Something was off… Not only that, but the change had happened so abruptly.

Finally, we stopped in at the guild to say hello.

"Natalie, good morning. I came to introduce my apprentice."

"Aaaaaaaaaaaaaaah!"

For some reason, Natalie leaped up from her chair and backed away.

*What's with that reaction? You'd think she'd seen a monster…*

"Um, I'm Akikana, an elf apothecary… I look forward to doing business with you…"

"Are you the one who was manufacturing Nutri-Spirits in Hrant?"

"Oh my, you know about that! That's impressive. Really, I'm truly touched you've heard of me all the way out here."

Hastily, I jabbed Halkara with my elbow. The fact that she made Nutri-Spirits wasn't in our script!

"Oh, right… Um, the elf who made Nutri-Spirits is a distant relative of mine. Her name is Halkara, and she's a silly girl, the type who eats poisonous mushrooms by mistake…"

Halkara began emphatically trying to cover her tracks.

"Is that right…? You see, this morning, an adventurer stopped by the guild. He said if we saw a person matching this description, he wanted us to let him know."

The paper Natalie brought out was the wanted poster Halkara had shown me (although this one had been translated from Demon into Human.)

I AM LOOKING FOR HALKARA, A FEMALE ELF APOTHECARY WHO MADE A PRODUCT KNOWN AS NUTRI-SPIRITS IN THE PROVINCE OF HRANT. AT PRESENT, SHE HAS GONE MISSING.

DESCRIPTION:
A VERY LARGE BUST.

I WILL SEND A GENEROUS REWARD EQUAL TO FIFTEEN MILLION GOLD TO WHOEVER FINDS HER.

DEMON BEELZEBUB 💀

"Aaaaaaaaaaaaaaaaaaaaaaaaaaaaaaaaaaaaaaaaaaaaaaaah! It's spread-iiiiiiiiiiiiiiiiiing!!!!!!" Halkara screamed.

I wanted to scream, too.

Was this why everyone had been so focused on her? Had they been wondering whether she was this elf…? I was relieved we'd used an alias.

"Huh. An elf from Hrant. What a coincidence. Still, her name is different, so it has nothing to do with my apprentice Akikana. Mm-hmm, yes, I'm glad she's completely uninvolved."

My strategy: bulldoze our way through this.

"I—I see… You're right…"

"By the way, where did the adventurer who brought this wanted poster go?"

"He just went around the village quickly, asking if there were any elves here. Evidently, he didn't think she was here, though. He's already set off for another village."

So we'd just missed him.

That was a small mercy, but word would get out soon enough.

We needed to come up with countermeasures, and fast.

Halkara and I left the village before noon and went straight back to the house.

I hadn't thought that poster would circulate this quickly...

My strategy of convincing people she was my apprentice might have backfired. Maybe I should have kept her hidden in the house for a while and introduced her as my apprentice later...

"First off, you're not allowed to go the village for a little while. We're fortunate there's no physical description going around, but given that very few elves live nearby, simply being one is enough to make people wonder. Hardly anyone goes in the woods, so if you want to exercise, you should do it there."

"All right... I'll be careful."

When we got home, Halkara was shaking like a leaf.

"W-will they come, do you think? Will Beelzebub's hunters come here?"

"Come on, pull yourself together. It's not as if they know what you look like. We can get through this. Try to be optimistic..."

Still, there was danger.

"Laika, could you evacuate my daughters to a distant village somewhere?"

"Yes, I was just thinking I should suggest that myself."

Having Laika around is a huge help.

"Please do, then."

I was planning to protect Halkara, but I also needed to make sure no harm befell my daughters. In cases like this, you couldn't call it a win unless you protected everyone.

"Mom, I want to fight, too."

Shalsha came up to me, seemingly deeply troubled.

"I tried to defeat you earlier, so this time, I'll make up for it and protect you—"

I hugged her tightly.

"Thank you, Shalsha. I appreciate the thought, but no. You're my daughter. Protecting you is your mother's job."

"But a book I read said that Beelzebub is really dangerous…"

At that point, Falfa came running up.

She took Shalsha's hand.

"Shalsha, you're causing Mommy trouble! Saying that makes you look like a dutiful daughter, but you're not being one at all!"

Even if she generally came across as childish, Falfa really was the older sister.

"All right…Sister."

Shalsha folded. Falfa patted her head. To their mother, the scene was truly adorable. I wanted to give some serious thought to the possibility of making a magic-fueled camera.

"Lady Azusa, our opponent is a high-ranking demon. It might be wise to further reinforce the barrier. Spells that repel demons have been handed down among humans, and I believe you could make one with your Spell Creation."

"Excellent idea, Laika. Now that you mention it, I remember reading about one in my grimoires."

"Then I'll return to my dragon form and take these two elsewhere. I'll be praying for your good fortune in battle from afar!"

"Yes. I know. Safe travels."

The three of them left the house quickly, flying away without eating the lunch waiting for them.

I wanted to apologize to Laika, who'd made enough for all of us, but right now, safety came first.

A little winged bug was flying near the neglected food.

It wasn't hygienic, and it just felt gross. I used my Ice and Snow spell to freeze the portions Halkara and I wouldn't eat.

I went outside and cast a demon-repelling barrier around the house.

"A high-powered demon might break through it, but if it wastes its power on that, I guess I can't complain."

My level bordered on cheating, too. This was likely to serve for the time being.

That afternoon and evening, nothing in particular happened.

*I guess they wouldn't attack us quite this quickly.*

"Sure would be nice if things stayed this quiet."

"Since long ago, it's been said that demons are nocturnal. It's possible they'll come at night…"

"Agh! If that's true, we won't be able to get a good night's sleep…"

No attacks came during dinner, either. The bug was still flying around, but since there was no insecticide in this world, I let it be.

After dinner, Halkara drank some Nutri-Spirits.

In a way, the stuff was the root of her predicament.

"Drinking it at night has become a habit for me…"

One bottle was pretty heavy, but Halkara had still come here with a dozen in her belongings. According to her, she'd drunk them to fuel her prolonged flight.

"Halkara, sleep in my room tonight."

"M-Madam Teacher, don't tell me you prefer women…?"

"It's because if you're far away, it will be harder to protect you! Obviously!"

I'm a sound sleeper, so it was possible the demon would attack Halkara while I slept. This was a move to prevent that.

"Y-you're so right… That was rude of me. I apologize."

We managed by moving Halkara's bed into my room. Sleeping in the same bed probably wouldn't have been a good idea. It would have been just plain cramped anyway.

Halkara talked loudly in her sleep that night, and I didn't get much rest.

"Huh? Melon sized? No, you're exaggerating. They're the size of large oranges at most. Ha-ha-ha... My rear end is peach sized. Kidding!"

*What on earth is she dreaming about?! Talk about being oblivious to danger!*

Nothing happened the next day or the day after that.

By itself, that was a very good thing. The trouble was that we had no way of knowing for sure whether we were in the clear.

How long were we to keep this up?

Halkara drank Nutri-Spirits that night, too.

A nighttime quaff was part of her daily routine. She said if she drank it in the evening, she could handle all-nighters... Although right now, she was spending all night sleeping.

"Aaaaaah! As long as I have Nutri-Spirits, I bet I could fight at night, too!"

Even if we did fight, my distinct preference was not to go up against Beelzebub.

"You really like that stuff, don't you?"

"When it comes to medicine, I work to create things I would personally like to drink. Besides, Madam Teacher, you're drinking it, too. Quite a lot of it, actually."

"Hmm? No, I'm not."

Relying on energy drinks reminded me of my office drudgery, so I avoided them.

"No, that isn't true. For the past several days, a bottle has been disappearing every day in addition to mine. I've run through my stock by now, so I'll have to make more from herbs for tomorrow."

"Huh...? But I'm really not drinking it..."

"Y-you're joking, aren't you?"

"No, I'm not. I wouldn't joke at a time like this."

Halkara and I looked at each other.

We'd both gone pale.

I had a very strong feeling we were in major trouble.

Just then, something flew toward us with a *buzzzzzzzzz*.

It was a winged bug. Come to think of it, over the past few days, it was like that bug had been in the room constantly.

When I took a closer look, I noticed that the insect was a fly.

I had an extremely nasty hunch.

"Say... Beelzebub is linked to flies, correct?"

"Yes. We've never met, but with a nickname like Lord of the Flies..."

"This is just an idea, but...........................could Beelzebub be that fly?"

Fearfully, I pointed at it.

"I-it couldn't be... That's just a dirty fly. They're nasty creatures that swarm over horse manure... Not a hair-raising demon like..."

"Who's a nasty creature?"

"Madam Teacher, don't speak in such strange voices! You startled me... Save your jokes for more peaceful times, if you would!"

"Huh? I didn't say anything. I'm not too good at doing voices, either."

"Then that voice— I-it can't be..."

Halkara's eyes went to the fly, too.

Since it was buzzing around, it was tough to keep a steady gaze on it.

"Correct. It is I."

Then, in a little poof of white smoke—

—a girl with the visage of an extremely distinguished lady knight appeared.

She was wearing something that reminded me of a skirt, but with the slits, the garment turned out to be more like a leotard. She was equipped with a leather belt and a sword, too, so she didn't have the bearing of a young noblewoman.

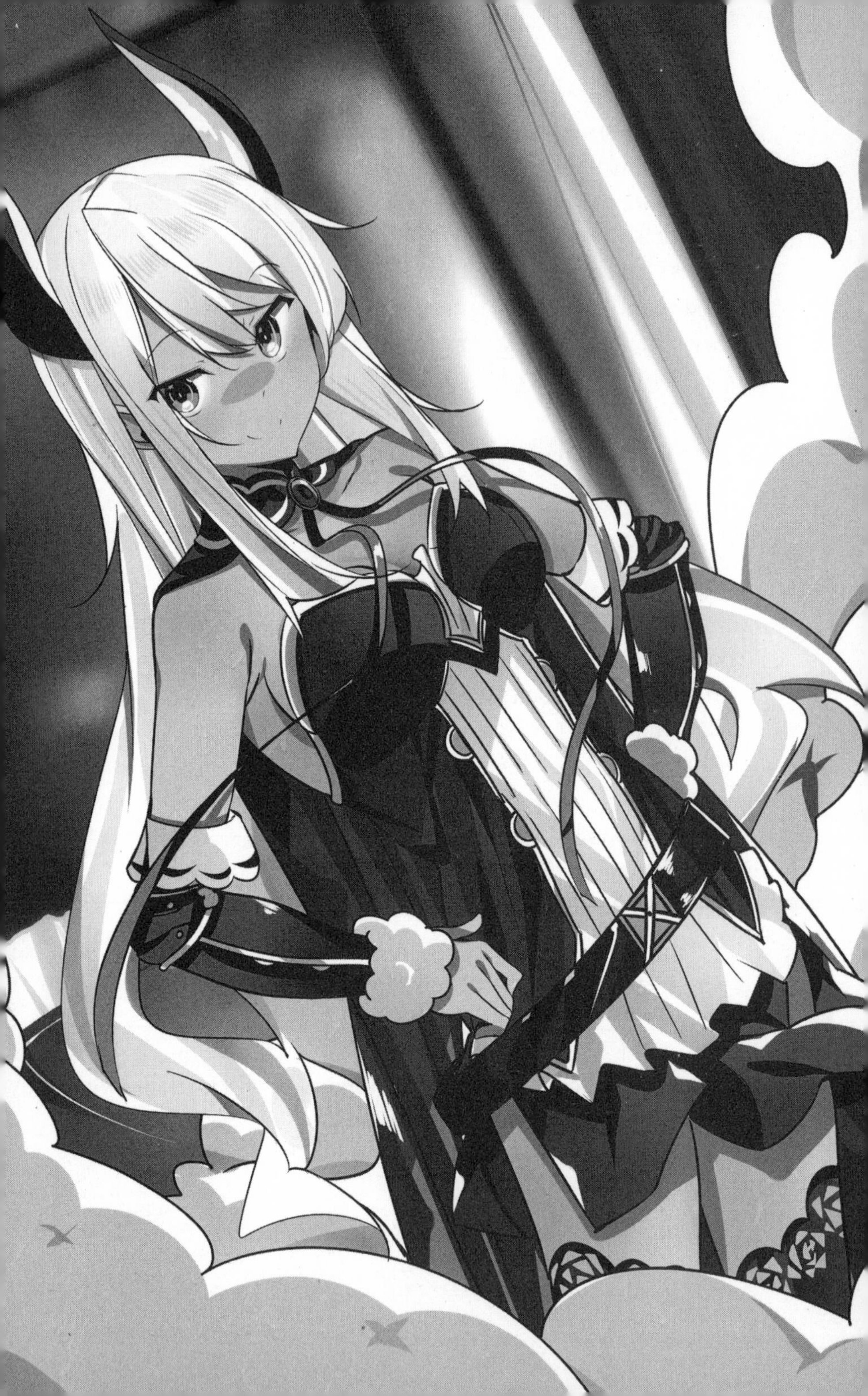

*Who is this character, and why is she cosplaying as an evil female military officer?*

As far as looks went, her most noticeable feature was her horns. She had long silver hair that struck a contrast with brown skin.

To all appearances, she looked to be close to my own age, which would have made her roughly a high schooler.

However, in my current worldview, it was pointless to guess someone's real age based on presentation, so it wasn't clear whether she was younger than me.

"My name is Beelzebub. I'd wager further introductions are unnecessary this late in the game, yes?"

To think she'd show up in person...

So Beelzebub was female?

When a name is that weird, it's hard to tell whether it sounds feminine or masculine at all.

"Yes. I can transform into a fly, and thus I am known as the Lord of the Flies. I'm sorry they are such nasty creatures. Allow me to apologize."

Beelzebub put a hand to her chest, bowing courteously.

Was she the type to listen to reason? No, she was definitely being sarcastic.

Besides, in situations like this, it's almost a solid rule that the more politely someone behaves, the tougher and more malicious they actually are. We couldn't get careless.

"Eee... Eeeeeeeeeep... *Nasty creature* was a figure of speech... I had no intention of saying such a thing to an exalted personage such as yourself, Lady Beelzebub... N-not the teeniest, tiniest..."

Halkara was ready to keel over from shock.

Actually, her legs had given out on her, and she'd sunk to the floor right where she was.

"No, no, you may call them such if you like. Although if that's the case, I do wonder about an elf who's terrified of such 'nasty creatures.'"

"E-elves are like dust... Th-they aren't even worthy to be food for anything e-e-e-eeeeeelse..."

*I know you're trying to survive, but you're really throwing elves under the bus here!*

"I did come all this way in pursuit of that dust, though."

Beelzebub whipped out a magnificent feathered fan and waved it at herself.

The sweet scent of fruit spread through the room. Was it because of the thing she was fanning herself with?

"I'm partial to the aroma of ripe fruit, you see, so I've perfumed this fan with its fragrance. And I don't mean the smell of rotten fruit. I don't enjoy the stench of rot, understand? Don't conflate the Lord of the Flies with common, filthy flies."

*It's hard to tell whether she identifies with her namesake or not.*

"You've been lurking in my house this whole time, haven't you?"

I hadn't calculated on being invaded this quickly.

That said, I had gotten Laika and my daughters out of harm's way, so that part was all right.

"Correct. The rumor that there was an elf here reached me right away. Flies love rumors and redolent fruit... And definitely not rotten smells."

*Does it bother her that people say flies like rotten things...?*

"Never mind that—why didn't you show yourself immediately? You were already in the house, weren't you?"

"That is how I spend my long vacations, buzzing lazily around houses in the form of a fly."

*Well, that's one way to enjoy your downtime!*

"The two of you finally noticed me. My vacation was just about to conclude, so your timing was perfect."

*Don't relish your time off in other people's houses without permission. I'll charge you hotel fees.*

"Now then, Witch of the Highlands. I have no particular business with you. After my long journey, though, I would appreciate it if you would bring me tea. Even so, you are not my servant, so I leave the decision in your hands. The one I do have business with is—"

Beelzebub's cold gaze went to Halkara, who was still paralyzed with fear.

"—Halkara. You fled from me, and I went to great pains to find you. However, it was trouble worth taking."

"Yee… Yeeek! Sp-spare me! I-I'll do anything!"

"Hmm, so you will do anything, will you? I heard you say it."

*Oh. This routine ends with* Then die!

There was no getting out of it. After all, temporary though the arrangement was, an apprentice is an apprentice.

I stepped in front of Halkara, arms spread.

"If you want to deal with my student, go through her teacher, all right?"

I smiled fearlessly.

There was nothing funny about the situation, but that was why smiling was all I could do.

Meanwhile, Beelzebub looked a little put out.

"You mean to hinder me? Are you obstructing my path? I'm surprised you have the nerve for that."

"I don't think my apprentice wants to see you. Can I trouble you to leave?"

"Is it not common knowledge that when one is told to go home, she wishes to stay?"

Transparent wings grew from Beelzebub's back.

They were beautiful, but their shape made them insect-like.

"This is perfect. I haven't fought in a long time and was getting rusty. I hear you have some skill. Fight me."

"I trained by killing slimes for three hundred years or so."

"Only three hundred, hmm? Well, well. That's about a tenth of my lifetime."

Apparently, the enemy was three thousand years old. *Yeah, you lived for three millennia, but I've eaten Chinese food. There's four thousand years of history in that!*

So this was bound to work out somehow.

I'd managed to get her to fight me.

Now I simply had to win, and everything would end peacefully. I'd never fought a high-ranking demon before, but I'd just have to take the plunge.

"U-um, Witch of the Highlands, I mean, Madam Teacher... A-are you sure...?"

I shot a glance behind me.

"You're an apprentice, so just sit tight. It's a supervisor's job to take responsibility for her subordinates' mistakes."

However, since this particular customer wouldn't settle for an apology, we'd have to resolve this physically.

"Listen, Beelzebub? If I win, don't retaliate by sending in your underlings, all right?"

"I would never do such a thing. This is a personal matter. That's why I came all the way out to this hinterland by myself."

"Oh, that's good to hear. In that case, I've got nothing to worry about."

*Now I'll just beat Beelzebub, and we'll all live happily ever after.*

"I'm displeased by your assumption that you will defeat me..."

"I mean, we won't get anywhere unless I do."

"If we fight here, we'll damage the building. Let us take this outside."

*Well, that's considerate of her. Much obliged.*

*I've got nothing to lose now.*

"All right. Let's both fight fair."


Once we left the house, I used Levitation to travel to the emptiest tract of highland I could find.

As if I'd let anyone destroy my house after we'd just expanded it! I planned to keep living there for a long time yet.

Since it was nighttime, it was very dark except for the hint of moonlight that illuminated the ground.

In a way, it might have been perfect for Beelzebub.

This situation suited devils much better than bright sunlight did.

"Oh-ho, you've flown rather far. All right, I suppose I'll go to you, then."

Even at a distance, Beelzebub's voice carried well.

She beat her wings to fly toward me.

That was when I remembered something.

"That demon-repelling barrier is still up..."

"Now I shall show you just how terrifying the power of an eminent demon can bagh-buh-buh-buh-buh-buh-buh-buh-buh-buh-buh-buh-buh-buh-bbbuh-buh-buh-buh-buh-buh-bbbuh-buh-buh-buh-bbbaaaah!"

Screaming like a broken CD player, Beelzebub got zapped!

"The barrier's working!"

Who'd have thought it would be so effective from the inside...?

Nevertheless, my opponent was a high-ranking demon. She punched through my spell and made it over to me.

...But she was glaring daggers at me, teary-eyed.

"Witch, you said we were fighting fair! What was that?! Do you intend to claim that as a strategic victory?!"

"Oh! ...Um, I didn't think you were already inside the house when I cast that, and, uh...I'd completely forgotten about it... Um, sorry."

I was aware I'd nearly committed a foul, so I bowed apologetically.

"Hell's bells... You've killed my enthusiasm for this... *Hff, hff...* C-come now... Let's fight..."

Beelzebub swayed on her feet as she spoke.

"Um! Aren't you exhausted?!"

The barrier had done its job far too well, albeit accidentally.

"Th-this is nothing.........*koff, kaff...* I feel sick..."

Beelzebub fell to her knees.

"I am so cold all of a sudden...and rather nauseated..."

Those symptoms were bad enough to warrant calling an ambulance!

"It's hopeless… I can't move anymore…"

There was no help for it, so I picked Beelzebub up. I went with the princess carry.

"I'm taking you back inside!"

"Don't! You'll hit the barrier again!"

"……That was close. I almost killed you…"

I'd genuinely forgotten. If I won that way, I'd probably be swarmed by higher demons looking to avenge her death…

"Oh, talking makes my head throb…"

"I'll take the barrier down, then bring you in!"

And so I ended up carrying Beelzebub back to my house.

"Oh, Madam Teacher! If you're back, that means you w— Agh, Beelzebub's here, too!"

"I'm putting her to bed! Come help me!"

Thus I ended up administering emergency treatment to Beelzebub.

I gave her some medicine right away, but something with a more dramatic effect would probably have been better. She still seemed to be in terrible pain.

"Ghk… I've never heard of a barrier so…ludicrously powerful…"

*So that's the power of a level-99 barrier…*

"Say, Halkara, can you use recovery magic?"

"No, I know nothing about it…"

"I can't use it, either. Recovery is a spell for clerics anyway… All right, I'll make one!"

I have Spell Creation, the ultimate spell.

I lined up a makeshift altar and some promising-looking leaves by Beelzebub's pillow.

It looked a bit like a sacred Shinto rope barrier, but it was nothing that auspicious.

Since this spell wasn't in my field of expertise, I was emphasizing atmosphere.

Now I just had to chant.

"O gods of the wide world, bestow creation's guidance on this— Wait."

In some games, using a recovery spell on a demon inflicts damage.

"Halkara? Is it okay to use healing magic on demons?"

"I—I think some demons can use them. I would assume it's probably safe…"

"All right! I believe you! If she takes damage from this and dies, it's your fault, Halkara!"

"It's what?! That's too much responsibility!"

Just to be on the safe side, I changed the chant.

"Gods of the wide world, your chaotic power has not yet been divided into good and evil. Imbue me with that power… HAAAAaaaaaaaaaah!"

Pale-blue light shone from my hands.

Beelzebub's color improved a little.

"It worked! Great, I'll repeat it!"

When I'd chanted the recovery spell five times—

—Beelzebub's face no longer looked pained.

"The nausea has subsided… As has the chill."

"Whew. That's great… All right, now rest, please."

I used my arm to wipe the sweat from my forehead. I'd just saved a life.

"I believed you to be an underhanded woman, but perhaps I was mistaken… Witch of the Highlands, you are rather venerable…"

"If you'd died on me like that, I have no idea how many centuries I'd have to live with the regret."

Apparently, I'd won her trust. Maybe this would work out peacefully.

Halkara appeared relieved as well. If she apologized properly, she was likely to be forgiven.

"Once I have recovered, I'd like another drink of those Nutri-Spirits."

"No, drinking those would put you right back at death's door."

"At death's door? Nay, I should probably take care not to over-indulge, but drinking them will not kill me. On the contrary, one drinks it to energize."

"Huh?"

This was weird.

That was not at all like the story I'd first heard from Halkara.

"Wait, what? I'd heard that you developed a high fever and nearly died after you drank it."

"Oh, I took the elixir during an all-night work session, and it filled me with zeal. True, I relied rather too heavily on the momentum, then collapsed and came down with a fever, but that was because of the strain on my body, not the drink. As long as I rest, I foresee no problem."

"Um... Then you were chasing Halkara because...?"

"They told me production had been halted, so all I could do was go to the manufacturer directly and request she start making it again. However, she had disappeared, so I sent out a missing-persons notice."

I tapped Halkara lightly on the shoulder.

"Hey. (Angry)"

"Oh! Um...I'd heard a rumor you'd collapsed with a high fever and had a grudge against me... Ah, you really do have to fact-check these things, don't you...? Ha-ha..."

Take care with your information...

When dawn broke, Beelzebub got out of bed.

Although she was still recovering from her illness, it was probably safe to say she was healthy.

"So you believed I'd kill you? I am a high-ranking demon, so I am accustomed to frightening people, but I had no idea such a rumor was circulating."

"I got desperate and ran... I'll start operations at the factory again, so… So wait, when the Nutri-Spirits disappeared from the house over the past few days, that was…"

"I helped myself. It is truly sublime."

Halkara and Beelzebub seemed to have resolved their misunderstanding, so let's call that a happy ending.

"Actually, maybe I'll relocate my factory to this province."

Halkara seemed to be considering something.

"Move here? But why?"

"Well, even if the story about Beelzebub hunting me down was a misunderstanding, both the elves and my home province did abandon me. At the very least, they made no attempts to protect me."

They'd probably gotten cold feet, since they were up against a powerful demon.

Maybe they believed sacrificing one elf would be a small price to pay.

"If I reopen my factory there, they'll get my taxes, and that just doesn't sit right with me."

"You're the type who holds a slow-burn grudge, aren't you…?"

That said, if it boosted employment in Nanterre, it might not be so bad.

As far as I was concerned, as a resident, promoting things that would help the province prosper was probably the right way to go.

"Also… If I live here, I'll be able to be with you, Madam Teacher."

Halkara blushed a little as she spoke.

"Wasn't our teacher-apprentice relationship just a front? You're a full-fledged apothecary in your own right, and I have no intention of driving you hard as my student."

"But you see, you really did try to save my life, Madam Teacher. When you stepped between Beelzebub and me, you were terribly gallant. And so, even now, my feelings are uncertain…"

Halkara's gaze was oddly fervent, and I was getting concerned.

"Halkara… You wouldn't be having any of those, um, Sapphic ideas, would you?"

"I have nothing of the sort."

"In that case, I suppose it's fine."

"I'm just heteroflexible, that's all."

*Whoa! That's an oddly specific term!*

"W-well…we do still have rooms available, so you could stay. Only, we handle cooking, cleaning, and shopping by turns, so be sure to do your share."

"Of course! I'll work hard!"

*I guess my family's growing again.*

Two daughters and two apprentices. This had turned into a genuine witches' studio.

*I'll have to develop my pharmaceutical skills as a witch, too, or I'll end up embarrassing myself.*

"Hmm. That sounds rather fun."

Beelzebub was displaying intense interest.

"Um, an eminent demon such as yourself would never want to live in this cramped little hovel, would you…?"

If Beelzebub lived here, the neighbors would probably be afraid of us, and everything would be awkward.

"I have a proper residence and no intention of moving. However, I will stop by. I want to buy Nutri-Spirits, too. If I visit this elf, Halkara, I'm sure to be able to procure it."

True. Buying from the manufacturer was the safest way to go.

"Besides, Witch of the Highlands Azusa, we haven't settled our score yet. Next time, we fight without that barrier."

"Huh…? You're coming to fight me?"

"Be at ease; I do not wish to fight to the death. When one lives a long time, boredom is inevitable. Help me kill time. If anything else of note happens around here, call me."

"Call you? How would I contact the demon lands?"

"There is a spell that's perfect for summoning. If you do not know it, I shall teach it to you later. Indeed, 'twould be convenient for you to have…"

*How often is she planning on visiting?*

This was the kind of situation where if I didn't call her for a long time, she'd get mad and drop by on her own, wasn't it?

"Well anyway, we know it was all a misunderstanding, and that's good. Would you like to stay and eat with us?"

"Hmm, yes, I believe I shall. Why don't we carry the table outside and eat there? It's a splendid opportunity. It would feel more like a highland inn, and 'twould be rather exciting."

"That sounds like work, but it's not a bad idea. Let's do it."

And so we ended up having an elegant breakfast in the great outdoors.

I'd never met a demon before, so I asked her several questions about demon society.

Q1　What is demon society like at this point in time?
　　　"The same dynasty has ruled for the past several centuries. There has been no real attempt to invade human lands, so we are getting along peacefully. It is governed by the king and us high-ranking demons."

*...Meaning it's a perfectly normal country.*

Q2　What do you do, Beelzebub?
　　　"As a noble, I manage several manors, and within the dynasty, I promote the expansion of farmland as the minister of agriculture."

*So apparently, she really is important.*

Q3　Are you married?
　　　"D-don't ask such peculiar questions. That is an activity for races that age rapidly. I-is it a problem for you if I'm an innocent maiden...?"

*     *     *

*So despite her manner of speech, she's a maiden?*

**Q4** **What do you do in your life as a fly?**

"Do not mistake me: Just because I can turn into a fly, that doesn't mean I prefer to eat filth. If you put out such a thing as my meal, I shall consider it an insult to a demon minister and declare it an international incident! True, fruit is good when it's very nearly rotten, but I do mean nearly, not actually!"

*Better be careful with this one. I'll just make sure to treat her like an ordinary human.*

I thought I should probably contact Laika and tell her there was no longer any need to lay low, but she came flying back in dragon form while we were eating.

"I returned alone, quietly, to see how things were going, but it appears the matter's been resolved."

"It has indeed. You're welcome to bring the girls back. Actually, it will make things pretty hectic, but do you think I could ask you to do that today?"

This was a rare opportunity, and I wanted to introduce the rest of my family to the Lord of the Flies.

Beelzebub and my daughters hit it off marvelously, and they played house and— Of course they didn't. What they actually did was ask a lot of questions about demon history.

"And thus, that noble line fell. But why are you so interested in history?"

"Because there aren't many books about demons."

"My sister, Shalsha, likes studying history! I like math more!"

"Ah, I see. In that case, Falfa, I'll bring you a book about differentials and integrals next time."

I didn't really understand it, but they seemed to be having an intellectual conversation.

That night, as Beelzebub was leaving, she said, "I would like to adopt one of your daughters. Would that be all right with you?"

"I'm honored, but no."

And so the Beelzebub matter was settled without incident.

"Yaaaaawwn. Good morning, Laika."

When I entered the dining room, everyone else was already there. Laika was in the kitchen making breakfast.

"Good morning, Madam Teacher. It's unusual for you to rise so late."

That was Halkara. She was already up.

She was right. I almost never woke up later than she did.

"Good morning, Halkara. Well, I have days like this, too."

"Don't tell me you spent a sleepless night with Laika…"

"You have some seriously ingrained assumptions, don't you? I bought a new grimoire and was so engrossed in it that I stayed up late reading. My daughters are here, too, so be a bit more careful about what you say."

"Yes, Madam Teacher, I'm sorry."

She seemed to be genuinely contrite. Good.

"It's only that, you know, I'm still young, so I'm not sure how to put this… I want something like a love story. It doesn't even have to be my own romance. I want someone around me to fall in love!"

Halkara's appeal sounded hungry.

"By the way, you said *young*. How old are you?"

"Se-seventeen..........and two thousand five hundred months, give or take."

"That's well over two hundred years old."

Although, at three hundred, I had no right to talk.

"But you see, with elves, you practically still have baby fat at that age! But forget my age—isn't there any kind of romance around?!"

"Frankly, no."

Over the course of these three centuries, I hadn't had any experiences you could call romantic. None at all.

"In that case, what about you, Falfa and Shalsha? Are you in love?"

This time, Halkara turned to my daughters.

The two of them had been alive for fifty years, but if either of them had told me there was a boy they liked, it would have been a bit of a shock.

"I love my mommy!"

"Th-that's about what I think as well…"

*That moment when your daughters say they love you is priceless. It really makes me glad I'm alive.*

"Um, no, that's not what I mean. Haven't you ever fallen in love with a man? Or, I mean, a woman would be fine as well."

"Listen… Would you please not teach my daughters weird things?"

"But, Madam Teacher, that has the opposite effect! Knowing too little about romance may end up wounding your daughters. Besides, from a human perspective, it wouldn't be strange for them to have grandchildren at this age."

"Erg… That's a pretty good point…"

True, I had no basis for assuming my daughters would never fall in love.

Still, they looked like they were about ten years old… Given that, wouldn't it be better not to teach them anything untoward?

"Mom, what are you worrying about?"

When I'm troubled, Shalsha always responds immediately.

"I'm wondering how I should explain what love is to you."

"Love is the gods' most magnificent gift to humanity, according to theology."

"Um, hmm, that may be correct in theory, but it doesn't feel quite right."

"In addition, when love is born, superficial feelings of pleasure manifest. This pleasure, however, is not love. On the contrary, it's more like a mist that obscures love, and one must take care not to be led astray by it. That is the theological interpretation."

*Hmm? I seem to be the one who's learning about love now.*

"Recent trends in theology suggest that love is divided into four types—*agape*, the absolute love of god; *storge*, the love of family; *philia*, the love of friends; and *eros*, romantic love—but that would take a while to explain, so I'll go over it later."

"Okay… Thanks…"

*Love really is complicated, isn't it? Not only that, but the topic of romantic love switched to a more general variety during this conversation. I do remember hearing something about love and romance being separate concepts… I'm getting confused.*

As I sat there looking agonized, Laika brought in plates of food.

"Here you are: scrambled-egg sandwiches. Take care not to burn yourselves, please."

*Of course. Maybe I'll ask about Laika's romantic experience.*

"Say, Laika, have you ever been in lo—?"

"Oh, Lady Azusa, there was something I needed to tell you."

Laika, who'd set the plates down, clapped her hands resolutely.


"I'm going home to my family."


For a moment, I gaped at her, flabbergasted.

"Wha-wha-wha-wha-what?! What happened?! Are you that unhappy with your life here?! If you have any complaints or worries, tell me—don't hold anything back! I'll fix it!"

I remembered when one of my junior coworkers had quit the company.

As one of their seniors, I'd advised them to hang on at least until they found their next job.

I'd actually died of overwork, though, so in a way, that junior's decision had been prudent. After all, if you're just going to kill yourself with effort, unemployment is the better option...

*This is no good. My memories are convincing me that quitting is a good idea.*

"Laika, was there a problem with me as a witch? Were my teaching methods wrong? Please, tell me!"

"Um, Lady Azusa?! What's the matter?"

"What else could it be?! I think of my apprentices as family! If you tell me you're leaving, I'm going to be upset!"

I truly was indebted to Laika. Our first encounter had been perilous, but now everything—even that—was a really fond memory.

"Lady Azusa, calm down a moment, please!"

"W-well, I can't, not about something like this... Don't quit being my apprentice, Laika!"

"I'm not quitting! My elder sister is getting married, and I'm simply going home for the wedding, that's all!"

"Huh? A wedding...?"

Come to think of it, when Shalsha attacked, Laika had mentioned that, hadn't she...?

"That's right. There's going to be a ceremony at Mount Rokko, the volcano where the dragon tribe lives. My sister is marrying her childhood friend. Oh, and they're both dragons."

Falfa was terribly happy and exclaimed, "Yaaaaay! Congratulations!" It certainly did warrant congratulations.

"So this is the shape of love?" Shalsha mused, sounding enlightened.

*Yes, I suppose you could say marriage is one of the ways to complete a romance.*

"I see, yes, definitely go to that. I'm sure your sister will be delighted."

"Yes. I'd like to celebrate the beginning of their new journey— Oh, that's right."

Laika seemed to have hit on an idea.

"Would you like to attend the wedding with me? There's no need to think about ceremonies or anything stuffy like that. Dragon weddings are fairly informal, so simply consider it something along the lines of a festival or road trip."

"I'm going! I wanna see the bride!"

My daughter Falfa expressed her interest before I did.

True, if this was the wedding of my apprentice's big sister, it would be okay for me to attend.

"All right. We'll go, then. At top speed, I think it would take about two days to get to Mount Rokko. If we take Falfa and Shalsha into account, we should probably pace ourselves and allow for four."

"I'll transform into a dragon and take you there. I'll arrange for your lodgings as well."

The matter was practically settled, then.

"A dragon wedding, hmm? We'll need to dress up… And I left all my dresses back home…"

Halkara already seemed to be thinking about what to wear.

"In that case, I'll make a trip back home ahead of time and let them know you'll be attending. I'll return later today."

"Of course. Give them our regards."

And so it was decided that the entire household of the highland witch would go to the wedding.


That day, we went into Flatta to have outfits made.

My daughters were already tremendously excited over getting to wear dresses. Their genuinely childlike reaction was a relief to me.

Shalsha tried on every frock in sight, constantly mulling over which would be best.

"Hmm, I don't think this one goes well with my hair..."

"That's not true. You worry about that too much, Shalsha."

"Well, Sister, you compliment every one of them, so I don't know..."

Going back and forth is part of the fun when it comes to this kind of thing, so I thought it fine that she was a little unsure.

Halkara had already begun trying on dresses off the rack.

"Excuse me, Madam Teacher? Could you come and tell me if this looks odd?"

She called to me from a changing room, so I went in.

"How is it? Did you find a good—? Oh, that one absolutely will not do."

Halkara was wearing a dress with a low neckline, and the moment I saw it, I knew it wouldn't work.

"Really? I like the color..."

"It barely hides either your bust or your derriere."

"......Oh! No, that's no good!!! I'll change!!!"

"Halkara, with your figure, none of the ready-made dresses will fit, and they'll all end up being provocative. Have yours tailored from scratch... And honestly, if you're planning to go in an outfit like that, I won't let you go at all."

She could stand to be a little more aware of how her own figure looks.

In the end, we had dresses tailored for all four of us.

Since Laika had gone to inform the people back home that we would be participating, naturally, she was absent. She'd been planning to attend the wedding all along, though, so she was probably ready anyway.

Laika returned before dinner. Apparently, our intent to make an appearance had been met with unanimous approval.

"My family said if the Witch of the Highlands was going to be there, they'd absolutely love to see you."

"I wish people wouldn't treat me like a celebrity."

"You are most definitely famous, Lady Azusa. I think the name Witch of the Highlands carries weight nearly everywhere in Nanterre."

I wanted to tell her she was exaggerating, but Halkara had come seeking my help despite living in another province, so my renown was probably real.

"We went to have dresses made. You already have one, don't you, Laika?" I asked just to be on the safe side.

After all, if she didn't, it might have seemed as though we were excluding her.

"Yes, several."

"Several? You do seem like a rich young lady... The ceremony won't be a problem, then."

"That's right. I'll be wearing a dress my sister gave me long ago."

What a pair of high-society siblings.

Very soon, the day arrived.

We dressed in our finest, Laika turned into a dragon, and we got onto her back.

Come to think of it, I'd never ridden Laika for such a serious distance before.

As a matter of fact, since my daughters had been evacuated during the Beelzebub incident, they were more used to it than I was.

Meanwhile, Halkara was looking pale.

"Are you afraid of heights?"

"No, it's motion sickness..."

"I don't think we're rocking enough to cause that."

"It's just how I am. There's no way around it... I'm hopeless unless I'm walking on my own two feet. During my escape, I rode on a riverboat, and it made me terribly seasick."

This girl has all sorts of problems—well, weaknesses.

"Here, I'll take some dried mushrooms that prevent travel sickness."
Mushrooms can do all sorts of things, can't they...?

*Halkara ended up getting nauseous anyway, so I had Laika
land in a forest temporarily.

I rubbed my apprentice's back. She was truly suffering, and I think
it's a genuine part of the job.

"That's right; get it all out. It'll stop hurting then."

"*Bleargh! Bleeeeh!* Ahh, I feel better. I'm sorry. My body really is
falling apart..."

"You don't have to beat yourself up over that. For now, just concen-
trate on calming down..."

My daughters seemed to be enjoying the unfamiliar scenery, so this
felt like the perfect time for a break.

"It's a forest! Shalsha, where are we?"

"This is the Forest of Mireille. Its altitude is relatively high for the
province of Nanterre, so it's especially green."

*That girl really knows her stuff when it comes to geography.*

"It's home to rather large 'long-spear boar' monsters, so people
don't often come here."

"Is that what that big animal over there is?"

At that, I flinched and turned. Sure enough, a boar with an incredibly long horn on its head was coming our way.

As I gazed at that large horn and wondered if it made life inconve-
nient for the creature, the horn extended farther. Evidently, they're able
to lengthen when the boar finds prey.

I realized right away that it was targeting my daughters.

"Sister, I may not be able to beat that one..."

"I don't think I can, either..."

Immediately, I ran to them.

"Don't you touch my girls, birdbrain! Oh, but you're a boar, so I
guess *birdbrain* isn't quite right... Anyway, get lost!"

I grabbed its horn, then launched it straight backward.

The move looked a bit like a back suplex.

Sensing danger, the fallen boar ran away.

"Whew. Do you think that did it?"

However, several other boars of the same species charged us. It seemed we were surrounded. We could have mounted Laika and made our escape, but...

"Say, Halkara? Are you feeling better now?"

"I—I think I'd like a little more forest air."

"Yes, okay. Laika, protect Halkara and the girls, would you?"

"Of course, Lady Azusa. Will you be all right by your—? Of course you will."

Laika was laughing, but, well, that was how it was.

There was no need to worry.

I slew five long-spear boars.

I say *slew*, but as our stop in a forest had been impromptu, I didn't have my knife with me. I just punched them.

This resulted in several magic stones, which meant these really were monsters, not wild animals.

"You've saved me again, Madam Teacher. You're so strong ..."

Halkara, now clear of motion sickness, spoke with a rapturous expression.

"If you kissed me, Madam Teacher, I don't think I'd mind... *Blush...*"

"You do remember you just threw up, right...?"

Needless to say, there was no kissing.

After that, we climbed onto Laika's back again and reached Mount Rokko without further incident.

Lots of dragons were gathered behind the mountain, the sort of place people wouldn't normally go. We could tell even from a distance.

"Woooow! Look at all the dragons!" (Falfa)

"Biologically, they're red dragons. They aren't monsters. They're classified as the dragon race." (Shalsha)

"If I anger them, I really will be killed this time..." (Halkara)

I did wonder why Halkara was always working from the assumption that she'd incur someone's wrath, but considering her life up to this point, that degree of worry was probably warranted.

"This is still the main party, so everyone's celebrating in dragon form. First, allow me to introduce you to the bride and groom and my family."

"All right. You're in charge, Laika. We'll follow your lead."

Finding an open space, Laika touched down, and we dismounted.

*To be honest, I can't even tell dragons' genders from a casual glance.*

The dragons' eyes turned to Laika.

"Lady Laika, how are you faring?"

"Your wings are as lovely as ever today."

*Why does it suddenly sound like a salon at a high-society girls' school around here?*

"What you're born with isn't important. What is important to us is the question of how to improve after we're born," Laika said, sounding sophisticated.

"Lady Laika, you're as classy as always."

Even her friends thought so. Since they were all dragons, this felt pretty surreal to me, but for them, this was probably normal.

"Thank you for attending my sister's wedding. I appreciate it very much."

"But of course we'd attend your sister's wedding, Lady Laika."

"That's right. Lady Leila took care of me when we were on the committee together. Well, you seem busy, so we'll take our leave. Let us chat again later."

The female dragons drifted away.

"I beg your pardon, Lady Azusa. They were my juniors at school."

"Oh, I see. School, hmm…?"

"We call it 'school,' but we only learn the basics there. After all, if one wants a serious education, it's much faster to adopt a human form and attend university."

"No, they seemed quite academic. I think I'm beginning to understand why you seem so intelligent, Laika."

"No, no, I can't hold a candle to you, Lady Azusa. I must continue to apply myself, that's all."

Come to think of it, in human form, Laika looks like she should be in middle school, so the other girls were probably about that age, too.

We traveled through the group of enormous dragons. I wasn't worried at all with Laika walking ahead of us, but if she hadn't been, this walking-among-dragons business would have been terrifying.

"They're all huuuge!"

"Sister, *huge* might be rude. It's true they are big, but…"

Shalsha and Falfa seemed excited. On the other hand, Halkara kept her eyes on the ground as she walked.

"If I anger these ladies and gentlemen, they'll kill me instantly… They'll breathe flames and turn me to cinders…"

I thought she was being incredibly pessimistic, but I could understand her difficulty relaxing with dragons all over the place.

Here and there, the guests were drinking liquor and eating from gigantic cups and plates.

The plates held sliced meat (although the pieces were too big for a human to eat) and vegetables.

The vegetables were served in batches of five cabbages and similar fare. These were most likely similar to bite-sized cherry tomatoes to them.

"Take care not to get onto any of the plates, please. You might be eaten along with the food."

Laika cautioned us from the front of the group. *Yes, I'll be careful about that.*

Immediately after the warning, Halkara accidentally got on top of a plate, then screamed, "Aaaaah! No, it's a mistake! I'm not food!"

"With all the dragons in the village here today, it's lively, but this place is usually a bit quieter and more laid-back."

"Hmm. About how many dragons live here?"

"Roughly two hundred fifty, perhaps?"

"That's a lot..."

"However, some ordinarily live on other mountains as well. Not everyone is from here. Also, that number only references our species. It's different if you include others."

"There are all kinds, aren't there?"

"Yes, and it's ludicrous that some of them are called 'dragons' at all— Oh, there's my parents, my sister, and her husband."

Four dragons stood there.

Two of them were big, and two were smaller.

The bigger ones were probably the males.

As I looked around with that in mind, I began to be able to distinguish their genders by size.

"I've just returned. This is my teacher, Lady Azusa, 'the Witch of the Highlands.' Behind her are her daughters, Miss Falfa and Miss Shalsha, and another of Lady Azusa's apprentices, Miss Halkara."

"I'm Laika's father. I've heard a lot about you. I hope my daughter isn't causing trouble for you."

The dragon who'd spoken was the largest of the group.

"No, no, I'm very much in her debt. I apologize for barging in on you like this."

"More guests have come to celebrate my daughter's wedding. How could that ever be a problem? Ha-ha-ha-ha!"

Guess they really were glad to have us.

Then Laika introduced her sister-dragon: "This is my elder sister Leila."

I said "Good afternoon" and bowed. My daughters and Halkara bowed as well.

"My husband and I were childhood friends for ages. When we reunited after eighty years, we really hit it off and decided to get married."

"Eighty years" sounded like an odd length of time for that, but it was probably normal for dragons.

"So everyone really is staying in dragon form for the ceremony…"

It seemed like that would result in an awful lot of spending on the food, but if this was the norm, it probably didn't strike them as unusual.

"We stay in dragon form for the main party, then switch to our human forms for the after-party and beyond. Being too large is unhelpful for delicate tasks."

The sister explained things for me. *Ah, I see.*

"Still, today really is nice and peaceful, isn't it?" the father dragon murmured.

"I hope it remains so all the way to the end."

Why say something that will so obviously trip a flag?

"Um, excuse me… Do these things ever *not* end peacefully?"

Frankly speaking, I didn't want that to be the case.

"Well, you see, the dragon race is divided into several tribes that live separately. Some don't get along, and they occasionally drop in to cause trouble."

So the dragon community had its own nuisances.

"In particular, when there's a wedding, there's a chance they'll crash it. Probability-wise, it's less likely than rain, so we can't waste much worry on it."

"I see. I do hope it stays peaceful, then."

"Dear, we must set out meals small enough for our human guests."

I assumed the dragon who'd spoken was the mother dragon. As I'd suspected, she was one of the smaller ones.

"Oh, you're right… Let's have them eat what we've prepared for the after-party at the mansion."

The father dragon ambled off, and we followed.

He took big steps, so if we didn't trot to keep up, we'd fall behind.

"I'm sorry, Lady Azusa. Father isn't very used to living with humans, so he doesn't understand how walking should feel."

"No, it's fine. It just means we have to keep our pace a bit brisk."

However, when we'd put some distance between ourselves and the rest of the gathering—

—the clear sky suddenly darkened.

I looked up and nearly screamed.

It had been blotted out by countless dragons.

Unlike Laika's and the others', their skin had a bluish tint.

"It's the blasted blue dragons. They've come for trouble!" the father dragon yelled.

"Blue dragons? Those exist?"

"Yes, madam. The blue dragons who live in the province of Heynt are shameless, barbaric wyrms who spew cold air all over the place…"

The dragons up in the sky suddenly exhaled white breath.

The trees they struck froze over as if it were midwinter. That really did look like cold breath.

They kept blasting the area ahead of them with it.

The wintry zone was gradually expanding.

"Aaaaaaah… I can't take this anymore… It's too hard on my heart. I want to faint…"

Halkara sank down, her face ashen.

"We can't have you fainting here. Get up!"

*This is getting ugly*, I thought, and just then, the blue dragons slowly descended for a landing.

There seemed to be about twenty of them.

One of the gatecrashers spoke. She was standing at the very front of the group, apparently the leader.

"Keh! Keh-keh-keh. Red dragons of Mount Rokko. I heard you're holding a wedding today. I came to harass you because it's so irritating!"

The dragon had just flat-out admitted that this was harassment. She hadn't even bothered to give a pretext.

"The idea of marrying when you're hardly a shade past three hundred! Why, I've been single for over four centuries!"

*I detect jealousy!*

"Not only that, but twenty years ago, when I proposed to my pearl dragon boyfriend at a get-together, he was like, 'You're the leader of the group bullying the red dragons, aren't you? I'd really rather not get involved with that mess...' and turned me down!"

*That's called 'reaping what you sow'!*

True, nobody wants to date somebody who devotes themselves to pestering people.

"All of that is my fault!"

*And she frankly acknowledged it!*

"Even so, in retaliation, I'm going to continue persecuting you! The hearts of blue dragons are as cold as freezing air! I sent a separate group over to the mouth of the volcano in addition to those of us at this wedding! We'll freeze that for you, too!"

*What a pain in the neck...*

"Her name is Flatorte. She's known as the harassment queen of the blue dragons."

The father of the bride offered an explanation for our benefit. Dealing with someone like that really would wear on you...

"There's no help for it. Now that it's come to this, we'll just have to have an all-out showdown with them."

Father Dragon had apparently steeled himself.

I heard the sound of heavy, scrambling footsteps, and when I turned, the dragons on our side had already started mustering. When a flight of dragons this big attacks, it doesn't take long to notice.

Laika went to shield her big sister.

"Sister, it's dangerous here. Please retreat with your groom!"

"This battle started because of us, so I'll fight!"

"I'm fighting as well, to protect Leila!"

Naturally, the newlyweds were dragons, too, and so they intended to engage. This was turning into a major incident.

Meanwhile, my top priority was protecting the ones who'd come with me: my daughters and Halkara.

"I'm scared, Mommy..."

Falfa clung to me tightly.

Shalsha gripped the edge of my dress, toughing it out.

Slime spirits couldn't hope to measure up to this many dragons.

For some reason, Halkara was already lying on her stomach.

"Why are you on the ground?!"

*There's no way she's been attacked already!*

"I-I'm playing dead. My grandfather's dying words were 'When you meet a dragon, play dead,' so..."

I was just about to inform her that was actually more dangerous when a running dragon left a heavy footprint right next to Halkara. One meter to the side, and she'd probably have been crushed and killed instantly.

"N-no more playing dead." Halkara got up, white-faced.

"Yes, I think that's probably wise."

"Please escape somewhere safe, honored guests. This is a fight between dragons. We'll finish it ourselves!"

No sooner had Father Dragon spoken than he charged into the fray himself.

*"Somewhere safe"... Where would that be?*

The cold breath came our way.

*Yikes!* I held up my right hand and unleashed a Flame spell.

Flames and frigid air clashed, canceling each other out.

As a result, we experienced nothing worse than a temporary drop in temperature, like a burst of air-conditioning.

"Mommy, that's amazing! But it's scary..."

"Mom, we're right in the middle of the battlefield. We should get farther away..."

Shalsha's suggestion seemed like a good plan.

I held the girls' hands firmly.

"Just leave this to your mother, you two!"

I hadn't asked to be level 99, but...

...right now, I was going to use my power to the fullest!

The dragon battle had heated up dramatically.

The combatants huffed breath attacks at each other and inflicted physical injury by striking with hands and tails. Since both parties had huge bodies, the fight was vaguely ugly and confusing but the potential damage they could do was terrifying.

Slowly, gripping my daughters' hands, I attempted to get away from the center of the battlefield. If I'd been on my own, I wouldn't have minded joining the fray, but if they took a direct blast of cold breath like that earlier one, the lives of my daughters and Halkara would be in danger.

Every so often, stray blasts nearly hit us, so I blocked them with fire.

"It sounds like this is simple harassment and no one's seriously trying to kill one another, but they're all dragons, and the scale is enormous. If ordinary humans got involved, they'd just die."

"Ahhhh... I can't do this anymore... My legs are quaking, and I think they're going to freeze up..."

"If you stop moving, you die. Walk, even if you have to force yourself."

"A-all right..."

Halkara was on the verge of tears, but I needed her to tough it out. There was no other way.

Now then, the question was, Where would we actually be safe? At this rate, backing up would be better than going forward.

That said, the blue dragons had charged into the rear of the venue here and there, too. Since our opponents could fly, they were naturally able to circle around behind us.

The party plates were getting flipped over and stomped.

Hmm. This was pretty exasperating.

I could understand simple envy of someone else's happiness.

Unless you're a saint, everyone feels like that sometimes.

But actually breaking things was unforgivable.

You shouldn't actually kill the normies with fire, and you shouldn't trash parties.

I wanted to yell at them to stop screwing around like this. Actually, I wanted to join the fight.

That said, protecting the noncombatants came first at the moment. This was no time to leap into the bloody, violent fray.

Slowly, slowly, we retreated.

Laika was spitting out flames and fighting alongside the bride and groom.

As I would have expected from someone who'd challenged me to a fight, she could hold her own. She was probably the strongest of the red dragons.

She was so good that, although female dragons were significantly smaller than their male counterparts, she was managing to take on two males at once.

"Fight well, my apprentice."

We migrated to a grove of trees that was still nearly undamaged.

"Falfa, Shalsha, you should be all right here, so wait a little longer. I'll save you, I promise."

"Uh-huh. I'll be patient..."

"You're a good girl, Falfa."

Falfa was desperately fighting back tears.

"Mom, I'm sorry we're making you worry."

"That's nothing to apologize for, Shalsha. You haven't done anything wrong, have you? Don't feel you have to when it's not necessary."

Shalsha tended to be a little too serious. Still, right now, saving them was the important thing.

Halkara was muttering, chanting something that sounded like a strange Buddhist sutra.

"Halkara, what's that?"

"It's a charm handed down among the elves. It lets you reach your destination safely without being attacked by animals in the woods, and it never fails. My grandfather said nobody who's chanted this has ever encountered dangerous beasts in the woods."

*I wonder if this is the other-world version of suddenly becoming religious in times of trouble…*

A blue dragon landed right in front of us.

Not only that, but it was an uncommonly large one. Its gaze seemed somehow sharp and cold.

"You people are friends of the Mount Rokko red dragons, aren't you?"

"And what if we are?"

"I'll rip off one of your legs right here. If you get hurt, it's bound to completely wreck the red dragons' wedding."

Something in me snapped.

"Sorry, but this is going to hurt a—"

"Listen, you. Are you seriously planning to frighten small (fifty-year-old) children just to pester someone? It's a bad sign when your brain works that way at your age, don't you think? Just what kind of hopeless, bottom-feeding life are you leading anyway? What have you lived for all this time? You gonna brag to people like, 'I scared tiny children!' or something?!"

By nature, I tend not to get worked up, but for the first time in a long while, I might have lost my cool.

"Huh? Well, I mean, that's what we came all the way out to this mountain to d—"

"You know that's no reason!"

I closed in on the dragon rapidly, raised a leg—not caring that I was wearing a dress—and kicked him.

*Thwok!*

The dragon's face warped in obvious pain.

Of course, that wasn't enough.

After all, this guy had actually declared his intent to hurt my daughters.

As a mother, there was no way I could condone that.

This time, I punched him with my right hand.

*Krakk!*

It was a combo attack that gave him no opportunity to strike back. I wasn't about to let him go on the offensive.

"O-ow... Wh-what are you, woman...? What kind of trick is this?"

*Trick? There's no trick.*

*I'm just level 99, that's all.*

Using Levitation, I rose until I was even with the dragon's face, then kicked it over and over.

I finished with an uppercut to the side of his nose.

Apparently, I'd given him a concussion, and the dragon hit the ground.

For now, I'd gotten the noncombatants out of danger.

This dragon was already unconscious and drooling and probably wouldn't be up to fighting for a while.

"Mommy, you're tough! Woooow!"

"I really respect you, Mom..."

"Thanks, you two. If you cheer for me, I'll get even more into this!"

Just then, an idea occurred to me.

There were no enemy dragons in the grove beyond us.

In other words, if I overwhelmed all the enemies, absolutely no harm would come to my daughters.

*All right. Guess it's time for a little rampage.*

If all they wanted was to bully people, crushing them wouldn't upset me whatsoever.

I'd inflict emotional scars they wouldn't forget for a century or two. They'd pay dearly for angering the Witch of the Highlands.

"Halkara, take Falfa and Shalsha and go hide somewhere."

"A-all right! Wait, Madam Teacher, you're going out there?"

"It's fine. I won't let a single enemy dragon come over here."

I grabbed the tail of the dragon I'd beaten.

It wasn't completely impossible he'd wake up, so I thought I'd take him along.

Lugging the dragon, I ran toward the battlefield.

Not much time had passed, but the uproar had expanded.

Technically, since this was a fight between dragons, that was only natural. At that size, it was hard to miss.

Ditching my blue dragon luggage in an appropriate-looking spot, I used Levitation to close the distance quickly.

"I'm taking out all these blue jerks!"

If you aim for their faces, dragons are easy to defeat, I'd just learned.

I launched Flame spells at the dragons' mugs with gusto.

"Waaaaugh!" "Eeeeeeek!"

They screamed. If you go for the face, even humans will flinch. *Sorry, but I'm showing no mercy.*

In lieu of a greeting, I hurled fire.

Some of the dragons spewed cold breath at me, but it was a dumb idea.

After all, I was blasting flames, so I was obviously capable of canceling it out.

If you think human fire spells are nothing to write home about, you're sorely mistaken.

For my finishing blows, I decided to rely on physical attacks. I'd considered using Lightning Attack spells, but it's incredibly hard to adjust the power on those. I thought killing somebody would be too much, so I wanted to strike the final blow a little before that happened. I was careful to avoid senseless killing.

As a rule, I struck at their faces, trying for a KO.

Since they were intelligent beings, an attack to their heads and the brains inside would probably petrify them and keep them from moving. Then I'd hit them with a flurry·of blows.

Three dragons fell heavily, and I was off to a promising start.

*Maybe I'll use a Wind spell this time.*

I soared up above the dragons' heads, then sent a whirlwind straight down onto them.

Buffeted by the maelstrom, two dragons crashed to the ground.

"Lady Azusa! Thank you very much!"

Behind me, I heard Laika's voice. She was soaring through the aerial battlefield.

"These jerks really got on my nerves, so I decided to thrash them. I won't be satisfied unless I punish them!"

Even as I spoke, I decked a new dragon. Punishment by fist.

People say that when you hit someone, it hurts you as well, but I didn't feel much pain. Besides, even if I had, I would have endured it. This was war.

"Laika, we've got to hurry up and finish things here, then head for the volcano. It sounds like they're attacking there, too!"

"All right! Thanks to your efforts, Lady Azusa, we have the upper hand here! If this keeps up, we'll win!"

Now that she mentioned it, the number of blue dragon combatants had dwindled. I thought I'd taken out about a third of them myself. *Well, sure, if we took down that many, things might work out somehow.*

We continued the clean-up, and then—

"What in the world are you?" a flying blue dragon suspiciously asked.

*Oh, this is the other side's leader.*

"You're, um, Flutter-Tail?"

"It's Flatorte! What manner of human are you? How are you able to physically beat a dragon?"

Since she was curious, I gave her an answer.

"It's like that saying 'Rome wasn't built in a day,' I guess."

"What's Rome?!"

*Oh, of course. She wouldn't know of any cities called Rome.*

"There's an ancient city by that name. Anyway, if you work at it steadily, even your physical attacks improve. It works the same way in video games, you know?"

"What's a video game?! You keep spouting nonsense!"

Fighting seemed to make the memories of my past life stronger. After all, back then, the only times I did battle were in video games.

*All right. Enough chitchat.*

Given the option, I wanted to take the boss character down in style.

I intentionally turned my back on Flatorte.

"I'm not letting you get away! We picked this fight, and we're going to win it!"

As if I'd run.

*On the contrary—I'm not letting you get away.*

I turned my hand toward myself and created a wind.

It launched me backward, and I closed in on my opponent.

Then, using the momentum from my air current—I sent a round-house kick into the bridge of her nose!

*Thwock!* A satisfying crack rang out as my attack struck home magnificently!

That wasn't enough to take her down, though. As you'd expect of a leader.

"Dammit! I'll freeze you!"

*Honestly. 'When all you have is a hammer...' It's all these people can do.*

With all my might, I sent a fire blast at the enemy.

My flames erased the cold breath, then struck Flatorte right in the face.

"Hot! Hoooot! I'm burning!"

*It's your own fault, you know!*

I soared up until I was above Flatorte's head, then descended in a rush.

"Witch Heel-Drop!"

The high heel I'd worn for the ceremony drove mercilessly into her head.

"Gah...hah..."

Flatorte plunged to the ground.

"I win."

The leader's defeat turned the tide, and the terrified remnants of the blue dragons fled.

"Well, I'd say it's safe to assume we've got them under control."

Slowly, I descended to the ground.

They may have been dragons, but they hadn't been all that impressive. Actually, being a small fighter against big opponents had ended up making things easier for me. I'd been able to accurately strike their weaknesses.

"Lady Azusa, you truly did the work of a dozen people out there!"

Laika rushed up to me, her hands free.

"Well, I was really just helping out—or maybe being self-reliant."

"Lady Azusa, do you think you could get onto my palm for a moment?"

Laika put out her large dragon's hand—on an animal, it would have been a front paw, but dragons are higher animals, so they use the word *hand*, just like we do. Obediently, I complied with my apprentice's request.

Then Laika held me up, in front of everybody.

I felt a bit like a pet hamster on display.

"Friends! Lady Azusa has done it! This is the power of the Witch of the Highlands!"

*I see; so this is like the victor's platform in an MVP interview?*

"I was watching, and she was truly astounding!"

"Long live the Witch of the Highlands!"

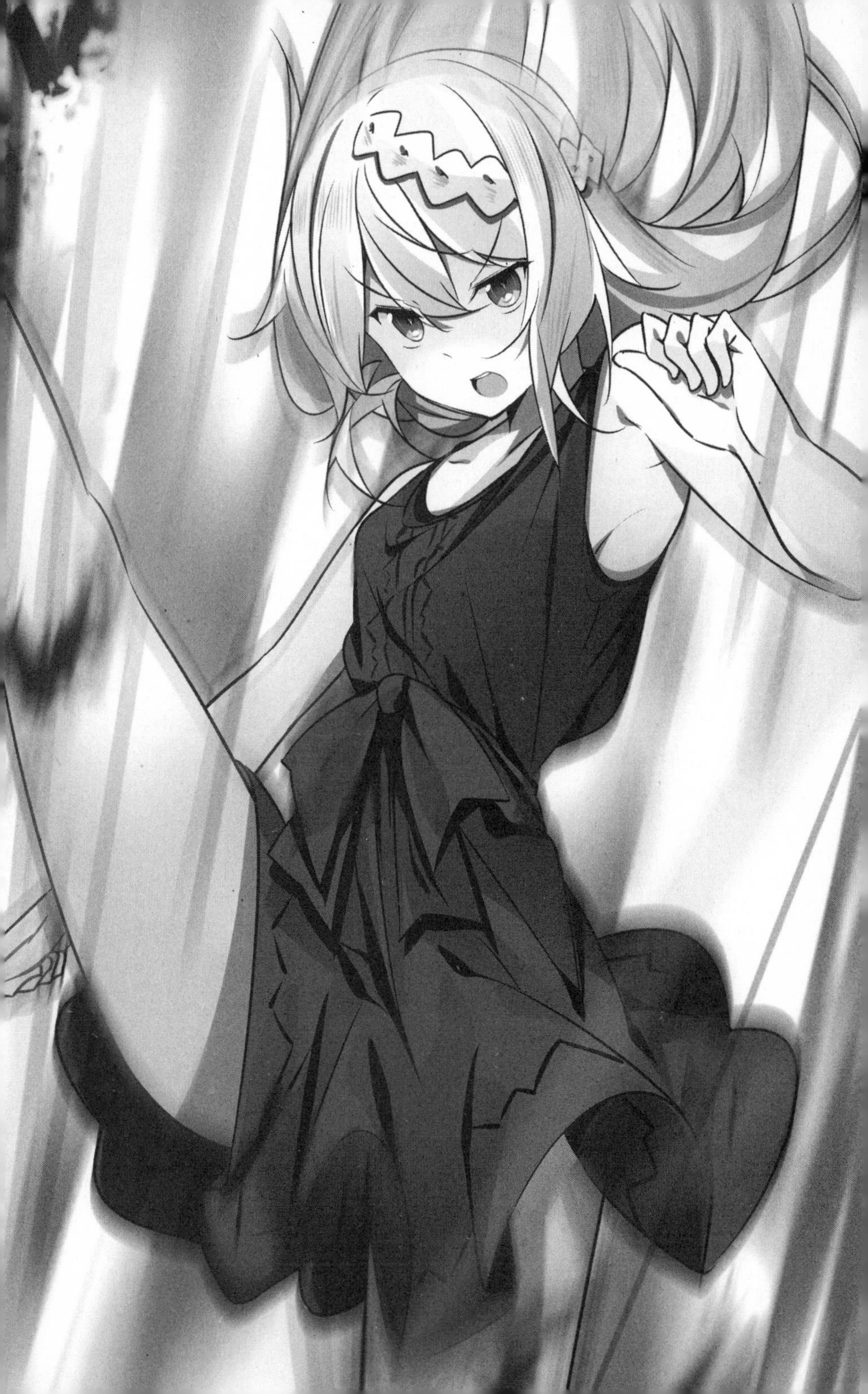

"I'd expect no less from the world's strongest creature!"

*There's absolutely nothing feminine about the moniker "world's strongest creature," so I really wish they wouldn't... Still, they do seem to be complimenting me, and that's nice of them.*

However, it was too early for the grand finale. The fight wasn't over yet.

"Now we have to go to the mouth of Mount Rokko. If they capture that, things will get unpleasant."

"You're right. Quite a few sightseers are up there as well, and there's a risk that ordinary people may be pulled into this. Not only that, but because of today's wedding, only a few dragons remain on hand, and I'm not sure whether they could fully protect it..."

*In that case, we really do have to hurry.*

"Laika, take me up to the crater!"

If the situation went south up there, the wedding ceremony would get even worse.

Conversely, if we managed to stop the damage on that end, we'd at least be able to continue with the nuptials. Since we'd won this battle, we could probably settle for "all's well that ends well."

"Yes, ma'am! Please get on."

Laika grasped me gently, then placed me on her back.

"All right, let's go! Dragons who can still fight, follow us!"

We took to the sky with Laika in the lead.

We were flying faster than we ever had.

When I looked back, about five dragons were following us.

Those numbers were probably good enough for now.

The crater wasn't belching too much smoke, but even so, it took quite a bit of courage to enter it.

"The inside of Mount Rokko is a large cavern, and many dragons make their home in it. It's also fairly common for humans with ties to the dragons to journey here."

True, as we advanced further in, a sort of human town came into view.

"When we host people such as tourists and government officials, we take human shapes and entertain them there, in surroundings similar to a human settlement. There are dragons who spend most of their lives in human form as well."

"I see. At a glance, though, I'm not seeing any signs of a battle in progress..."

We were getting closer and closer to the town inside the crater but found no indications that anyone had laid waste to it, and I didn't see dragons fighting anywhere.

"What? How strange... They can't have been annihilated already, can they?"

Laika verbalized the worst-case scenario.

*That would be too much. Please let everybody be okay...*

Laika landed on the outskirts of the town, and I got down off her back.

She assumed her girl form, and we searched the hamlet together.

It was virtually the same as its human counterparts. The main street was lined on either side by buildings made of stone or brick.

"It's unnaturally quiet."

"I think so as well..."

This was a completely unexpected development.

We'd assumed we'd find a ferocious battle unfolding here, too, yet it was eerily silent.

Unsettled by the situation, we traveled deeper into the town.

"I want to make my sister's wedding a good one, somehow... I want it to be a success..."

I heard Laika murmur quietly.

"It's all right. We'll end everything safely, and they'll be able to finish your sister's wedding."

I laid a hand on Laika's back, trying to reassure her as well as I could.

Just then, abruptly, I heard an unfamiliar sound.

"Uu… Ghuuuuh… Uuuuh…"

*What was that? A groan?*

It sounded like a dragon, but…

Uneasily, we went on, and then we met a shocking scene.

Five blue dragons lay sprawled across a plaza.

They didn't seem to have any strength left to fight. They were all lying limply.

A magic circle or something like it was shining below the plaza. Had this spell done that?

"Does this technically mean we won?"

"It does appear that way, but that isn't a spell I'm familiar with. I wonder who cast it…"

Laika seemed dubious. I didn't know what kind of magic it was, either.

"Is it a curse-binding spell to restrain one's enemies? No, that's not it. This leeched power from them, weakening them until they couldn't move. It's a nasty bit of work…"

While we were performing our on-site investigation, an acquaintance turned up.

"What, it's you? Fancy meeting you here."

When I turned toward the voice, there stood Beelzebub.

"Huh…? Yeah, this is an odd coincidence. What are you doing here?"

"Well, it is a tourist spot, as you well know. This crater is home to some excellent hot springs. I stop by once in a while to relax and soothe my fatigue."

A hot springs visit, hmm? That explained why Beelzebub was here, but…

"Um, what happened to those dragons over there?"

"They were being rowdy, so I taught them a lesson."

Beelzebub spoke as if it was nothing.

"I was taking a stroll through town when those wyrms showed up. They were spouting dunderheaded nonsense about kidnapping sightseers and lowering the place's value as a tourist spot. So I went out and smote them."

Beelzebub picked up a pebble, then chucked it at the immobilized dragons.

"This is a spell that causes extreme weakness. It's handed down only among demons, so you two may not know about it. Perfect for apprehending criminals, yes?"

"You defeated five blue dragons by yourself?!"

Laika sounded mystified.

"Hmm? Why would I be beaten by a paltry five? I can spit icier cold breath than they can. I'm a higher demon who's lived for three thousand years. I'd never lose. Honestly, don't insult me."

Beelzebub's face flushed red, and she looked miffed.

"You, too, Azusa. You don't believe I'm just another petty foe simply because you beat me with a cheap trick last time? Next time, when we fight fair, I cannot say how it will end! After all, I am strong!"

"Um, that doesn't matter right now."

"Wait, hold it! It cannot possibly not matter! It is of utmost import!"

I went up to Beelzebub and hugged her tightly.

"Thank you! You've averted a crisis for the red dragons!"

"Agh! Do not cling to me so! It's shameful! Besides, I didn't do it for you people. Those poor excuses for dragons were full of themselves, so I taught them a lesson, that's all!"

"Hmm? Beelzebub, you smell nice, like you just got out of the bath."

"That's because I did just get out of the bath—and that is not important! Unhand me!"

What I learned today:

Beelzebub > Dragons

We returned to the wedding venue right away and reported that all was well at the crater town.

With that, the battle was safely brought to a close.

As soon as I got back, I rushed straight to my daughters and Halkara.

"I was scared, Mommy!"

"Mom, thank you for coming."

"I was thinking about carving my last words into a tree…"

My daughters (and even Halkara) hugged me. Though, there was no room for the elf to latch on to me, so she reached around from behind and embraced that way whether I liked it or not.

"You didn't come back, Madam Teacher, and I was truly worried. I thought you might have fallen into the dragons' clutches. Falfa and Shalsha started worrying, too, because of me… We were beside ourselves."

*Whoops. That's another problem with getting back late, isn't it?*

"I'm sorry. I really didn't have the time to turn back."

"You had it harder than we did, Mom, so it's all right."

"You did come back, Mommy, so I forgot the sad things!"

I hugged my daughters tightly, over and over.

Cleaning up the rest also went relatively quickly, thanks to a certain someone.

Beelzebub cast that weakening spell on the blue dragons who had attacked the wedding and immobilized them, too.

Now there was no risk of a sudden second bout with these guys.

"Hell's bells… I came here for the baths. Why do I have to do odd jobs?" Beelzebub grumbled, but in the end, she did paralyze them all for us.

"Thank you. Now there's nothing to worry about."

"For hell's sake. If you make such shameless requests, it's embarrassing to refuse."

Little by little, I was learning how to manage Beelzebub.

She was the type who couldn't say no when people asked her for things.

…Although I did feel as though I might be a pot calling the kettle black.

Moving along, everyone wanted to resume the wedding immediately, but there was still one thing left to do first.

"All right. Time to pay up."

I was smiling, but this incident really had infuriated me. Some things are okay in this world, and some are not.

"Flutter-tart, switch to your human form. We'll have an easier time talking that way."

"It's Flatorte! Remember my name correctly, would you?!"

"Human, now. We're going to talk."

Reluctantly, Flatorte changed to her human shape.

Although her figure was human, unlike Laika, she had a dragon tail sprouting from the back in addition to her horns.

She wore a rather pretty pink dress, and her long hair had a purple sheen.

However, since the weakening spell was in effect, she was flat on the ground.

"I assume this is good enough... What do you want?"

I asked Laika to handle the actual negotiations.

"First, regarding the compensation for the damages of this battle, we'll be charging you this amount."

Laika, who was also in human form, showed Flatorte a piece of paper.

"Blerrrgh... Y-you want that much? Isn't that more than the cost of the wedding?"

"It includes compensation for mental anguish and for injured parties. Of course it's a lot. If you don't like it, would you rather be immobilized here forever?"

"Th-that would be a problem..."

Losers couldn't afford to complain.

"All right. I'll accept that condition."

Great. The bargain was struck.

Still, I wanted to take the chance to get one more thing settled. We just happened to have a perfect third party on hand for this.

Pulling Beelzebub after me, I went over to Flatorte.

"All right. There's another pact I want to make with you, in addition to the damages."

"A pact?"

"Right. A nonaggression pact between the blue and red dragons. Naturally, attacking for purposes of harassment is out of the question."

"N-no, but... I'll lose my reason for living..."

Maybe it's against the rules for somebody with no intention of marrying to say this, but this is probably why she's single.

"If you don't agree, you'll never go home again," I said to Flatorte, smiling.

"Yeeeeeeeek! Your smile is scary!"

"So agree, then. All right?"

"Fine... I'll agree to it! I will! So forgive me!"

"Lady Azusa... You were thinking about this?"

Right... I hadn't even told Laika about my plan yet.

"That should bring peace to Mount Rokko."

"Thank you so much!"

Laika thanked me profusely, and my mood improved a bit.

The pact between Laika and Flatorte was safely sealed. Laika's strength was top tier among the dragons, and her position let her act as the representative of her tribe.

I poked Beelzebub lightly.

"Your turn. Do it right."

"I know. I just have to say it, right?"

Beelzebub cleared her throat.

"Furthermore, I and Azusa, 'the Witch of the Highlands,' witnessed the conclusion of this pact. If the treaty is broken, you will dishonor both me and the Witch of the Highlands. Remember it well."

Flatorte turned pale. In a way, she looked ready to hack up a powerful blast of cold breath.

"There's no way I could ever beat the Witch of the Highlands and the Lord of the Flies."

"Of course not. We'd wipe out your pitiful blue dragons in five minutes flat. If you do not want that, then straighten up and live an upright life."

Flatorte held her head.

"I should never have done this…"

And so all the postbattle cleanup was safely finished.

The wounded blue dragons staggered home, while Flatorte stayed behind by herself to serve as a hostage until the damages were paid.

"Beelzebub, thank you for everything. We found a good compromise."

"You are the only one who could work the Lord of the Flies like a dog. In return, you must invite me to something fun."

"Yes, if we hold any events, I'll call you."

Beelzebub was a thoroughly good person.

"I'll be counting on you from here on out, too!"

I've always been the person people turned to, so it was a relief to have somebody I could lean on. While I was at it, I hugged her again.

"No need to cling so, much less over and over!"

Now all we had to do was get on with the wedding.

## FALFA AND SHALSHA

Spirit sisters born from a conglomeration of slime souls. They've been alive for about fifty years. Falfa, the older sister, has a childlike, carefree personality. Shalsha, the younger one, is mature and reserved. They both love their mother, Azusa.

## HALKARA

A young elf woman and Azusa's second apprentice. She's seventeen years and 2,500 months old. She has a figure anyone would envy and a brilliant mind that made her Nutri-Spirits a hit…but she's rather lacking in several other respects.

## BEELZEBUB

A high-ranking member of the demon elite known as the Lord of the Flies. She's been alive for three thousand years. Her personality is belligerent, as you'd expect from a demon, but she's actually about as good at looking out for others as Azusa.

The main ceremony was in shambles after the blue dragons had crashed it, so the wedding began with the after-party.

However, in dragon weddings, there were no actual rituals—such as an exchange of vows between the bride and groom—so it wasn't that big a problem.

So, on to the after-party...

Basically, it was totally different from the reception.

After all, it was held with all participants in their human forms instead of their dragon ones.

The after-party took place in a spacious building intended for events. The round tables were piled high with mountains of food. Still, given the size of the dragons I'd seen at the main party, this seemed sensible.

The lively crowd of horned, chatting dragon-people were making short work of their meals.

If you'd said it was a perfectly ordinary buffet-style party, you would have been correct... Although everyone was consuming extraordinary portions.

Even the older folks were polishing off enough for five people.

Laika was probably constantly holding back, too. If she'd tried to eat more, she probably could have.

We set to work on the food as well, but there were so many different types that we were stuffed before we could sample the whole spread.

"Mom, my tummy's full…"

Shalsha was the first to drop out, so Falfa took her over to a chair by the wall. I was proud of her for acting like a proper big sister.

Falfa ate quite a lot herself. Since the twins ate different amounts, you'd think their figures would have been different, but they looked the same. Maybe it was because they were spirits.

Halkara ate way more than I'd expected her to.

"For some reason, when I eat, it seems as though the nutrients go to my chest and rear," she'd said.

She didn't overeat and make herself sick, but she ended up in trouble on another front.

"Woooow, this liquor is reaaaally stiff. C'n barely stand up…"

She drank something alcoholic and ended up plastered almost immediately.

As she swayed and stumbled, she kept eating, but the only ending I could see for this was all that food coming right back up.

"Honestly. The creation of Nutri-Spirits is that elf's sole saving grace."

Beelzebub was scarfing down a heaping plateful of spaghetti.

"Demons eat a lot, don't they?"

"Partaking of delicious food is the key to good health."

I thought you were beyond worrying about health once you'd lived for three thousand years, but going out of my way to point that out would probably have been gauche.

As a dragon, Laika ate the most of all of us. This was a buffet, and just from what I'd seen, she was on her seventh plate.

"You look insatiable for a human, but this is normal to you, isn't it, Laika?"

"I'm hungry because I fought, so this is a bit more than usual."

Evidently, the concept of dieting doesn't exist for the dragon race.

I've been talking only about the food, but of course, there was more to it than that. After all, this was a wedding.

"Lady Azusa, let me introduce my sister and her husband to you again."

In human form, the bride and groom were a lovely couple, an attractive man and woman.

The bride was a beauty who resembled Laika—after all, they were related by blood—while the groom's chiseled features could have made him a Hollywood star.

"Lady Azusa, Lady Beelzebub, it's thanks to you that we have been able to proceed with our wedding. My wife and I are both grateful to you."

"Really, thank you very much. Please continue to lend your support to our red dragon tribe."

In response to their courtesy, I immediately bowed my head. "No, no. I only helped you out a little, that's all..."

"I see you are well aware of your place. If you continue with your adulation, I suppose I could lend you a hand again."

Beelzebub put her hands on her hips, striking a triumphant "Ahem!" pose.

"You're being too arrogant! Modesty, modesty!"

"What for? I *am* great, so what is wrong? This is normal for me. ♪"

*Great! From now on, I'll manipulate Beelzebub with constant flattery.*

Just then, there was a slight shift in the mood.

The blue dragons' leader had come over to us. She was holding a single rose.

"Oh, you're Cocoa Latte!"

"It's Flatorte! Why can't you remember my name?!"

Ah, right, she was being held as a hostage.

"Um...Leila..."

Flatorte stood in front of the bride and averted her eyes as she spoke.

"Congratulations. Be happy from now on."

Then she handed the rose to Leila.

*Hey, this blue dragon has a decent side.*

At first, the bride looked surprised, but she took the flower with a smile.

"Thank you, Flatorte."

"I lost this time. As the loser, I'll congratulate you sincerely."

Apparently, she wasn't a bad girl, deep down. I sensed something like friendship between them, as well as a long history.

"Yes, *Forever-alone* Flatorte. I'll be happy enough for both of us."

The bride offered a barbed reply.

"What's that supposed to mean?! I–it's not that I can't get married! There just aren't any good men!"

"Oh? And just how many times have you come to me, bragging about finding a good man or making a good match for yourself?"

Possibly having remembered something embarrassing, Flatorte was flushing red.

"Hmph! You know what, go ahead and divorce! If you have a kid, I'm not sending congratulations!"

Flatorte ran off to a corner of the venue.

"Looks like a complicated relationship, Laika…"

"The red dragons and blue dragons are rivals, but they aren't sworn enemies. It's a nuanced affair. It's possible you would need to be a dragon to understand this, but…"

*No, I think I get it, kinda.*

After that, Laika and I went to fetch what I'd set my sights on since the beginning of this after-party: dessert.

Dragon puddings, egg tarts, and cheesecakes are all rumored to be masterpieces.

*They say you have a second stomach for dessert, and I plan to eat heartily.*

"Oooh! There are so many delicious layers underneath this subdued sweetness! It's like a dream!"

Laika and I sat in empty chairs against the wall of the venue.

"Um, Lady Azusa, could I ask a favor…?"

For some reason, Laika seemed hesitant.

"Sure, what is it?"

"C-could I rest my head on your lap…?"

That was an unusual request.

"You see, it's something my elder sister often let me do long ago."

*Oh, I see.* This wedding had taken Laika's sister from her.

"Sure. You're welcome to rest your head in my lap as much as you like; that's nothing. Go on, lie down."

"I apologize for asking for something strange."

Shyly, Laika settled her head into my lap.

"I've always been more athletic and a better fighter than my sister, but I feel as though whenever something troubling happened, I always slept with my head on her lap. The firmness was just right…"

"I see. Your sister's married now, and asking a married woman for something like that seems a little mean to her husband. Is that it?"

"Yes, that's… That's more or less it…"

Laika sounded embarrassed.

Even if you always live bravely and earnestly, sometimes you just want someone to pamper you.

"You can think of me as a big sister instead of a teacher, if you'd like."

"No, this is an exception. Just for now…"

"In that case, take your time and enjoy this 'exception' to your heart's content."

*Come to think of it, I have daughters, but I don't have a little sister.*

*It might be nice to think of Laika as a sibling.*

Laika and I passed this curious little while together.

I've been alive for three hundred years, and it's probably all right to have times like this that are difficult to classify.

A hubbub rose from farther back in the venue.

When I took a closer look, Halkara was lying on the floor.

*What is that girl doing...?*

Falfa and Shalsha were calling to her, but she wasn't opening her eyes.

"Big Sister Halkara, wake up!"

"Miss Halkara, that's not very clean."

"*Hic*... Are you sayin' you can't drink my fruit liqueur...? *Hic*..."

Right now, she was the most conspicuous thing in the venue. She definitely drew more attention than the bride and groom.

*Look, try not to embarrass yourself too much, would you...?*

"Hell's bells, that elf is trouble."

Beelzebub went up to her and slung Halkara over her shoulder.

"I shall take you somewhere with a bed or a sofa."

*She really is a decent person. Are demons allowed to be this good?*

However, Halkara was too defective to receive a kind gesture without incident.

Her face suddenly went pale.

"Ughk... I feel icky... I'm gonna throw up..."

"Wha—?! Hey! Don't you throw up on my back! Don't you dare!"

Beelzebub had blanched as well.

"You can say that, but it's definitely coming up..."

"If you do, I'll tear you limb from limb and burn you to ashes, body and soul!"

"I-I'm going to die! Oh, oh no, this is really bad! Ughk, uugh!"

"Bathroom! Where's the bathroom?!"

In the end, the two of them disappeared into the restroom.

Halkara was not murdered, so they probably made it in time.

At the end of the after-party, everyone sang a song to bless the bride and groom. It was a cheerful dragon folk tune.

At that point, I thought it was about time for us to head home, but...

"Since you are here, will you not stay in the inn at the crater?" Beelzebub suggested.

"Hmm? Come to think of it, you said there were hot springs here, didn't you?"

"Indeed. Actually, the hot springs are why I ventured here in the first place."

"All right, we'll stay!"

When I told Laika we wanted to stay as a family, she made the arrangements immediately.

Since I was the hero who'd quelled the uproar, they put us up for free.

$$\diamondsuit$$

At the moment, we were soaking in a hot spring.

As you'd expect from a volcano, the inn had several open-air baths. Not only that, but it was deluxe. Each room had its own splendid private outdoor bath.

"Falfa is really good at the breaststroke!" my older daughter exclaimed.

"All I can do is doggy paddle..."

My daughters were playing around in the spacious bath.

"Hey, no swimming— Actually, never mind. This is a private bath, after all. You can swim, but don't play so hard that you overheat."

"Okaaaay!" "Mm-hmm."

They'd agreed, so it was probably all right.

All the members of the group who weren't children were relaxing in the water.

"To dragons, this sort of bath isn't unusual, but it's fun to go with everyone this way."

Laika was sitting on my right.

"You're right. The water really is nice."

I'd fought enthusiastically today, too, and it was good to be able to soothe my fatigue away.

If you were wondering, Halkara was sitting on my left.

"A hot bath is a woooonderful way to sober up, isn't it? It feels so gooood..."

"It seemed like you were just getting in one bad scrape after another, Halkara, but all's well that ends well. Look on the bright side."

"Yes, I wiiiill. Hmm...? I seem to have gotten overheated..."

"So it didn't end well, either!"

Somebody reached in from behind us, pulled Halkara up, and laid her down on the rocks.

"For hell's sake. Just cool off there. We're outdoors, so you should recover soon."

Yup, it was Beelzebub.

"I'm pretty sure we were in different rooms, but no point in bothering about that now, I guess. There's an open spot by me. Come on in."

"Hmm. I shall."

Beelzebub took the seat Halkara had vacated.

"Being near you is fun. Never a dull moment, I'd wager."

"Not sure *fun* is the word I'd use for a lot of it. Still, you saved us this time. The town is safe thanks to you, Beelzebub."

"I told you several times already. I didn't vanquish those blue dragons for your sake. It merely turned out that way. You are free to express your gratitude if you so desire, though."

"Then I will. Besides, you probably would have helped if we'd asked you to anyway."

"W-well, maybe... Never mind that. Let me fight you one-on-one again."

"Yes, yes, I know, Sis."

There was a weird pause.

After I said it, even I was like, ...*Huh?*

"Why am I your sis?"

"Well, you help with all sorts of things if I ask you, and you're good at taking care of people, and... I'm not sure how to put it. You're just big-sisterish, so... 'Sis'... *Pfft! Snrk-snrk!*" After that, I laughed out loud.

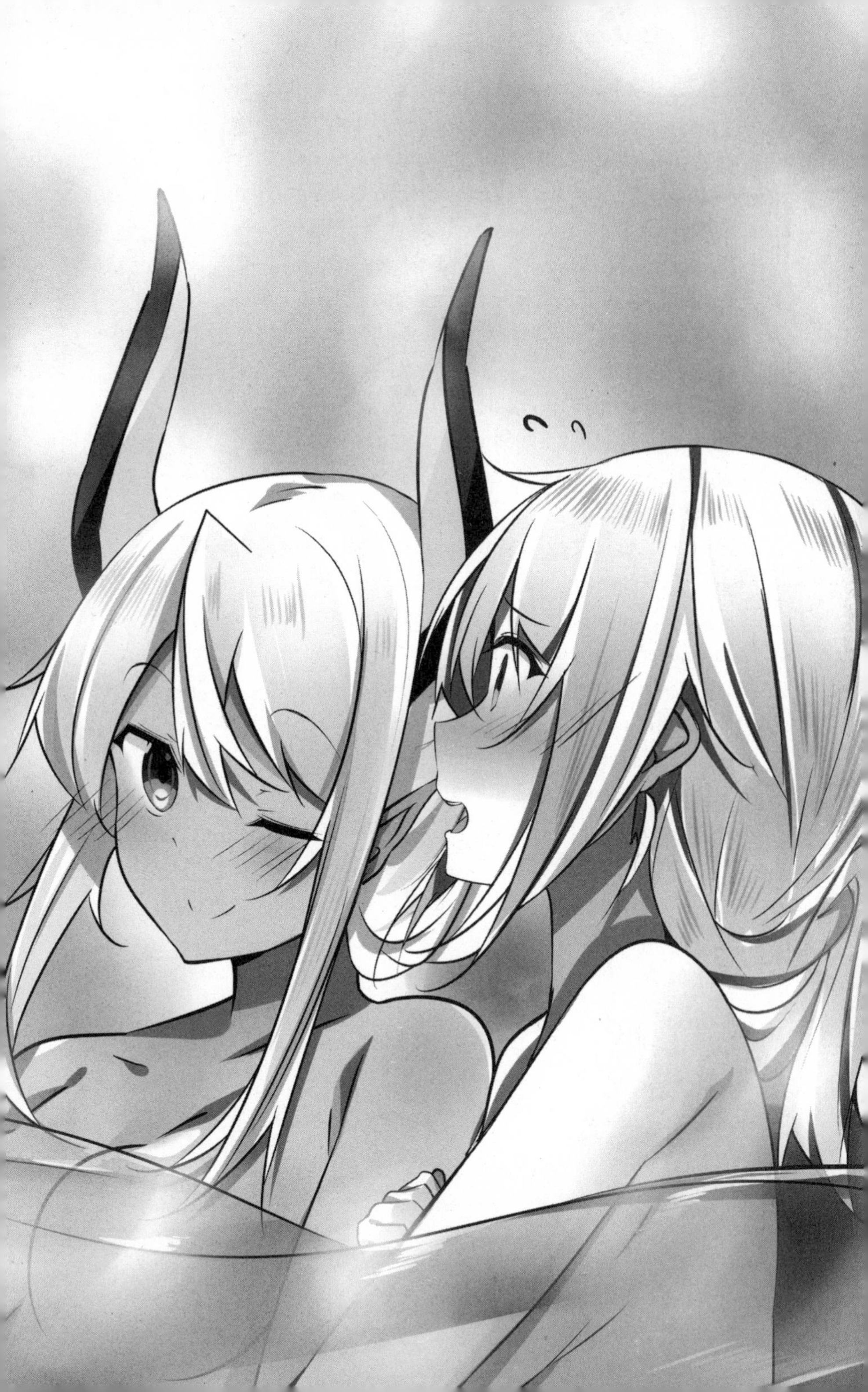

"Yeah, that's it. I have two daughters, Laika's my little sister, and you're my big sister, Beelzebub. That's not a bad family to have, is it?"

My laid-back life wasn't solitary anymore, but now that my family had gotten bigger, the more the merrier. A concept change for my three hundredth year.

"I'm your little sister…? I see…S-Sister."

"I'm delighted to hear you call me that, Laika."

"You are indeed my little sister, as one who provides no end of trouble. You are not mistaken."

Beelzebub sighed and nodded.

"Mommy, you look like you're having so much fun!"

"That's a great smile, Mom."

My daughters could tell I was happy, too.

"However, in that case, you've left one out, have you not?"

Beelzebub glanced behind us.

"Haaaah, the night wind is sobering me up and cooling me off…"

Oops. I forgot about Halkara.

Her apparent age made her look like a big sister, but I was actually older, and there was nothing big sisterly about her anyway.

"Halkara is…um…a junior coworker who's a handful?"

"Madam Teacher, that's not fair!"

Everyone except Halkara burst out laughing.

When you can't stop laughing, that's proof you have a good family.

"Come to think of it, what sort of place are you originally from, Falfa and Shalsha?"

That question came from Halkara, during breakfast.

We'd just been talking about the elves' forest in her home region.

"Belgria," Falfa answered immediately.

I'd never heard of a place by that name before.

"The deep forest of Belgria. It's said nobody lives there. There was an abandoned work hut, actually, and nobody was around. That was where we lived."

From Shalsha's comments, the place sounded fairly spooky.

"That sounds like fun. Let's go visit."

"Halkara, what about that story sounded fun to you?"

I really did think Halkara's values were skewed.

"Well, it's a forest. What elf would be frightened of the woods?"

I see. As far as elves are concerned, eerie or not, as long as it's a forest, there's no problem.

"I think I might like to go home for a visit, just a little bit…"

Shalsha looked down as she spoke.

"You're right. Falfa wants to see Great Slime, too!"

"Great Slime?"

That was an odd name.

"It's the biggest good slime in the world!"

Apparently, a special slime lived in that forest. Those woods had given life to slime spirits, so maybe it wasn't unusual for it to have a connection to slimes.

"In that case, shall we go on a day when the weather's nice? If you ride on my back, I think we can all go together."

Laika had agreed as well, so we decided to visit my daughters' birthplace as a family.

Traveling via Laika in dragon form, the forest of Belgria was about three hours away. Even if Laika was flying at sixty kilometers per hour, that meant the place was 180 kilometers away, which was fairly far.

The woods really were gloomy, and almost no sun filtered in. The tall trees blocked out the light.

"Oh-ho... Awfully dark, isn't it? Mushrooms that can survive in weak light are growing underfoot. How unusual..."

Halkara had discovered the mushrooms and gotten rather excited, but Laika, who was in her human form again, looked melancholy. "It's dreary and suffocating..." My own opinion was closer to Laika's.

"You two were born and raised in a place like this?"

"Yes, we were! It's great, isn't it?!"

"The quiet environment made it an ideal location for studying."

*I see.* Part of what had made them good students was the nature of the area.

This kind of spot would raise contemplative people, it seemed. Although, it did look completely uninhabited.

"Do you think Great Slime is well?"

"Great Slime just *is*. Concepts like 'well' and 'ill' don't apply."

Judging from their conversation, Great Slime was a deity or something.

"I wanna feel the Great Slime with my whole body!"

"When you become one with the Great Slime, you're released from worries and fatigue."

*Seriously, what is this Great Slime thing?!*

Then, when we'd walked through the woods for about twenty minutes...

...right in front of me, I saw a hill that shone and sparkled like an enormous jewel.

Even if no one lived here, it was hard to believe a gem of this size had been left untouched... What in the world was it?

"It's Great Slime, Mommy!"

"Huh? This?!"

"Now that you mention it, it does look like a slime. If you made it as big as you possibly could, it might turn out like this." Laika went closer and began to touch it, patting at it.

I did the same. It really did feel rubbery.

"Yaaaaay!"

Falfa shucked off her shoes and ran up the slime-hill.

Once she'd reached the top, several meters above the ground, she bounced for a bit, then rolled around. She bounced high when she jumped on the elastic surface, as if it were a trampoline, and since the slope was gentle, she didn't fall.

"It's like playground equipment..."

Copying her sister, Shalsha also took off her shoes, then slowly climbed up Great Slime. Evidently, removing your shoes was part of how things were done.

"Madam Teacher, what should we do? They both went up..."

Even though she'd been fine with the forest, the fantastic slime seemed to frighten Halkara, and she was acting a little nervous.

"My daughters would never take us somewhere dangerous."

We decided to follow the girls. We took our shoes off, just in case.

Stepping on the soft, flabby surface, we went up and up until we arrived at its smooth peak.

There, my eyes were opened to the splendor of Great Slime.

"This is so nice and cold!"

Yes, lying on top of this Great Slime was relaxing, cool, and pleasant.

"Lady Azusa, I think I may grow addicted to this."

Even Laika's expression had softened, which was unusual. But I couldn't do much about that, not when this Great Slime's power was enough to corrupt her.

As for Halkara, after about five minutes of lying on top of the Great Slime, she was fast asleep.

"When we got tired from studying and things, we came to Great Slime and took breaks," Falfa explained.

"Slimes should rest on top of slimes. It's the most logical," Shalsha added.

Whether or not it actually was logical was questionable, but there was no denying that Great Slime was valuable.

Still, this was, at its core, a slime.

It wasn't a sofa in a hotel lobby or anything of the sort.

I'd forgotten that.

In front of me, the ground—or rather, a part of the slime—welled up.

It shifted and solidified into a form that resembled a human woman.

"Wh-what…? What's this…?"

Involuntarily, I braced myself. In a way, this thing was more reminiscent of a slime spirit than Falfa or Shalsha.

"Oh, it's Great Slime!"

"It's been a very long time, ma'am."

My daughters greeted it. I see. This was an actual friend of theirs, too.

"I am so pleased to see you two, as well. And you've brought your family with you today."

Apparently, Great Slime was perfectly capable of speaking.

"You're Azusa, 'the Witch of the Highlands,' aren't you?"

She called my name abruptly, and I flinched. How did she know about me…?

"My name is Great Slime. I am an integrated thought entity, formed when good slimes gathered in order to protect themselves. As a result, the hearts of all the good slimes in the world are linked to me. I've known of your existence for a very long time."

*I guess she's at the top of the ladder!*

"Um…it's a pleasure to meet you. I am Azusa, 'the Witch of the Highlands'…"

I bowed so as not to be rude.

"Now then, up to the present, you have killed a truly vast number of slimes, haven't you?"

*Erk…*

I'd thought she might bring that up.

"Um…you aren't angry about that, are you…?"

*I guess she would be, huh? After all, she is a slime.*

"No."

Great Slime shook her head. It seemed I'd been forgiven.

"It isn't that I think nothing of it, but you've used the strength you gained from killing them for the good of the villagers, for your family, and for Falfa and Shalsha, who were born of the slimes' souls. Those were good deeds. Please continue to do them."

"Thank you very much."

This high-order being had given me her approval.

"By the way, your total human ability is ninety-four points."

I'd been assigned a mystery score, but it was high, so the matter didn't particularly bother me.

"Great Slime is an amazing being who can objectively award points to humans," Shalsha explained.

"Next, Laika."

When her name was called, Laika flinched, too. It did feel like getting called on by a teacher.

"Because you were known as the strongest of the red dragons, you were haughty. However, in order to achieve that position, you had to put forth unstinting effort, and after being defeated by Azusa, you have devoted yourself to further study. Your attitude is exemplary. Eighty-two points."

"Th-thank you very much…"

Laika had also gotten what could safely be called a passing grade.

"I'm happy for you, Laika. Great Slime has a good eye for people."

"Hearing that makes me self-conscious…"

I doubted she could just be openly proud of it, but even so, Laika didn't look altogether dissatisfied.

"And now, Halkara."

Great Slime turned toward Halkara, who was sleeping like a log.

"Halkara is………fifty-one points."

"Low *and* no explanation!"

One of us was clearly slacking off!

"It's true that Halkara has profound knowledge as an apothecary, and her real-world ventures into the forest and continued observation and investigation is worthy of a high evaluation. She also has a bright, energetic personality. Nevertheless, she is…scatterbrained…incomparably so…and causes trouble for others with incredible frequency, so… with the intent to encourage future improvement, I have awarded her fifty-one points."

"You're not wrong. There isn't a single mistake in there…"

Laika and I smiled wryly. Either way, the evaluation contained some affection, I thought. However—

"Great Slime, that's not right!"

Unexpectedly, Falfa raised an objection.

She went to stand in front of Halkara.

"Halkara is Halkara, scattered brain and all! If she was serious and careful and didn't make any mistakes, she wouldn't be Halkara! That would just be somebody else!"

The scales fell from my eyes.

She was right. That would be just like telling her, *Become a perfect superhuman.*

Certainly, if I were a company president and Halkara were my subordinate, I'd probably prefer a perfect superhuman—but she was family. There's something fundamentally wrong with demanding perfection from family members.

"Falfa likes the absentminded Halkara who makes mistakes! And that goes for everybody!"

Great Slime's eyes had been opened as well.

"I'd expect no less of one born from the gathered souls of slimes. To think you'd teach me a lesson…"

Great Slime smiled gently.

"Please continue to love and watch over Halkara. That is what family is."

"I'd do that even if no one told me to," I answered proudly.

In other words, I just had to do what I've been doing and act normally. We're a good family.

"Then, in closing, let me give you a word of advice, Azusa."

"Advice?"

"You believe that your thoughts reach each other. However, hearts can be stubbornly cryptic. For that reason, you would do well to incorporate a moderate amount of physical affection."

In general, I understood what she was getting at.

"You mean this, don't you?"

Laika was close to me, and I pulled her into a hug.

Great Slime was nodding, so that had to be the right answer.

When you only talked about family ties, the words were dubious and empty. There was something hollow about them. And so, in order to make up for that, we clung together as a family should.

Laika was like a little sister to me, you see. Nothing wrong with a big sister hugging her beloved little sister.

"L-Lady Azusa…"

It had been abrupt, and Laika was embarrassed. Maybe I should have told her what I was going to do beforehand. That would have been its own kind of awkward, though.

Besides, adopting a doctrine for physical affection was putting the cart before the horse.

We hug because we want to.

"I'm sorry. If you'd rather I didn't, I'll let go."

"No… Let's stay like this for a while…"

As far as I was concerned, Laika's embarrassment made her even cuter. She was also the right height for me to embrace as a big sister.

"Aaaaah! Mommy, hug Falfa next!"

Falfa bounced up and down, insisting.

I hugged my daughters frequently, but of course I didn't mind doing it more often.

"In that case, this is enough for me."

Laika pulled away. She was blushing. Diffidence is in her personality.

"All right then, I guess you're next, Falfa."

"But before me…"

Falfa tugged Shalsha's hand and brought her over to me.

"Shalsha wants a hug, too, so do Shalsha first!"

To think she'd be this considerate of her little sister! Falfa was a model older sibling.

Shalsha didn't say anything aloud, but she indicated what she wanted with a small nod.

"Okay, come to Mommy one at a time, then."

Timidly, Shalsha came over to me. I bent down slightly and held out my hands.

I'd been living with my daughters for a while now and could tell the difference between Shalsha and Falfa in my arms.

Naturally, I don't mean I'd analyzed them bit by bit or anything like that. The one who melted into me gently was Shalsha, and the one who grew more cheerful as I hugged her was Falfa. It was the differences in their personalities.

Shalsha closed her eyes and quietly nestled into me.

It was like she was trying to listen to the sound of my heart.

"Thank you, Mom."

Speaking calmly, Shalsha turned her eyes to Falfa. Did she mean *Switch with me*? Great Slime was also gazing at my daughters warmly.

"Mommy, I love you!"

Falfa flung herself at me.

I was level 99, and I caught her firmly. It was a straightforward, unclouded expression of love.

"I love you, too!"

Now I'd hugged everybody, except for the sleeping Halkara—or so I thought, but Halkara had woken up and was eyeing me steadily.

"Madam Teacher, I'm welcome, too, aren't I?!"

Hugging Halkara would mean hugging a mature woman, which would be a different kind of embarrassment from the others, but I shouldn't discriminate.

"Yes, yes. You can come over here, too, Halkara."

"Thank you very much!"

Halkara held out her arms.

The sensation was definitely unique.

*Those are breasts…*

They were pleasantly elastic, but they also seemed to cleave to me. It was like I'd felt something similar just a moment ago…

*Oh, I see! Great Slime!* The cushiness of the enormous creature and Halkara's breasts were nearly the same!

"Great Slime, it's like a cushion up here on top of you, but you've got the strength to bounce Falfa and the rest of us back up, too. It's very relaxing."

Beside me, Falfa was talking to Great Slime.

Yes, that same strange relaxation could be found in Halkara's bosom as well. It made me feel like a child again…

"Heh-heh-heh! You look rather defenseless and adorable right now, Madam Teacher."

I did think, *Apprentices shouldn't call their teachers adorable*, but it was true. It felt so good that I was actually leaning on her.

*Uh-oh. My mind is getting muddled.*

If something isn't done, I won't be able to resist Halkara…

"Hmm? I'm getting sleepy again, too."

Halkara mumbled a similar sentiment. *Okay, but you were sleeping up until just a minute ago.*

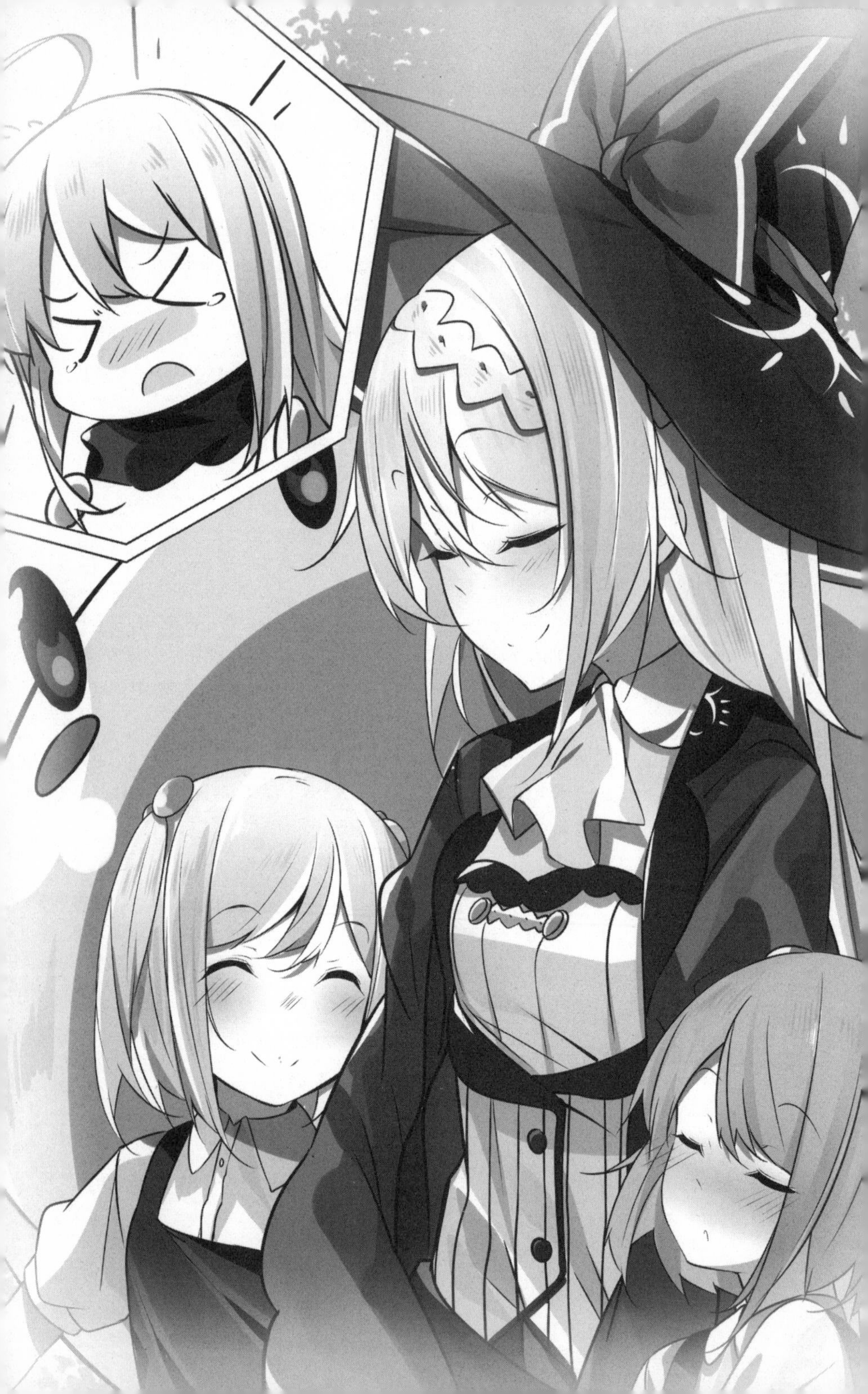

"Lady Azusa! Something like poisonous gas appears to be circulating through this area!"

After Laika spoke, she immediately covered her mouth.

"Huh? Poisonous gas?"

"Oh…! I'm terribly sorry. A fairly potent gas sometimes erupts in this forest. It's harmless to slimes, but it may be rather unhealthy for humans…"

Great Slime spoke as if she'd just remembered.

"It's not the kind that knocks you out cold, is it?! Instead of just making you sleepy?"

No wonder there were no people in the forest. You weren't supposed to come in here.

"Laika, take your dragon form!"

"Lady Azusa, you need to put your shoes on!"

"Mommy, Halkara looks like she's falling asleep!"

"Whatever you do, don't let her!"

We got onto dragon-Laika and booked it out of the forest as fast as we possibly could.

Next time we came, we'd be careful about how long we stayed…

*The End*

Thank you very much for buying *I've Been Killing Slimes...* et cetera! (I'll proceed under the assumption that you have indeed bought this book.)

It's a story in which a girl who's a former wage slave becomes an overpowered witch, occasionally fights enemies, and leads a relaxed, laid-back life along with other characters with eccentric backgrounds.

This novel earned its author, Morita, the top points for the day on the novel submission site *Shousetsuka ni Narou* (*So You Want to Be a Novelist*) for the first time ever. In other words, it hit number one in a single day.

Since it took first place a fairly short time after I'd submitted it, at first, I didn't really know what had happened. I had serious suspicions it might have been a dream.

Because everybody rated it almost before the story had gone any-where, I think the title *I've Been Killing Slimes...* must have had a nice ring to it.

I don't have any arcane anecdotes that would count as behind-the-scenes secrets, but this is an afterword, so I'll give it a shot.

One fine day, when I was walking through the neighborhood near my place, just before I reached an intersection, the phrase *I've been kill-ing slimes for three hundred years* popped into my head.

I thought if I made that the title of something, it might stand out, and I started writing.

…That's it.

I wish I could tell you a slime spirit spoke to me, but it wasn't a particularly mystical experience.

The thing is, it hit me just as I was passing the garbage dump site, so it might have been the work of a garbage spirit. I don't really want to meet one of those…

From now on, whenever I have some sort of crisis—if it starts to rain and I don't have an umbrella, or if it looks like I'm going to be late to a meeting, or if I've made curry but forgotten to steam some rice—I think I'll say "I've been killing slimes for three hundred years!" like a spell of sorts.

Fortunately, this book didn't end as a type of one-shot gag and was acknowledged by many people, and they've created a bound version of it. Really, thank you very much!

Now then, since this is an afterword, I'll write just a little about the underlying theme of the book.

In a word, it's "Working too much isn't a good thing."

Again and again, I've seen people who've run themselves ragged and sort of gone to the dark side because of it.

Fortunately, no one close to me has died of overwork, though some of them have gotten sick because they pushed themselves, and it came back to bite them.

I've had those experiences, and then when I was a student, I also interviewed with a company that worked to correct labor environments.

Of course, I've also seen many cases where not working at all isn't a good thing, either, so here's the bottom line:

I think the happiest situation is an environment where everyone can work in moderation, and if they can see that their work is helping others, then it's even better. This is the story I wrote as a result.

Needless to say, this is a work of fiction. If you walk through a real town, you won't find any actual slimes. However, Azusa makes a living by killing them in moderation, making and selling medicines in moderation, and I think—in moderation—that a life like that is just about right.

I wrote this messily, but it's a book about a girl who kills too many slimes and becomes so powerful it's practically cheating, so if you thoroughly relax as you read it, I'll be satisfied!

If you get into your bed and yawn while you read, I'll be happy. Please make it your Health Recovery item. Also, if it's interesting enough to keep you wide-awake, that would make me happy as an author.

In closing, some acknowledgments.

Thank you very much to Benio, who was in charge of the illustrations!

The laid-back, relaxed atmosphere of Azusa's family comes through in the illustrations as well! I'd like to kick back and take it easy in that house in the highlands, too! In particular, Falfa and Shalsha are so cute that it's almost criminal... I happen to be male, but they tickle my maternal instincts. I'd also like to drink sake and gripe with the (apparently) adult Halkara and Beelzebub.

In addition, to the people who've been kind enough to buy this book and provide their support, three hundred slimes' worth of thanks! It's no exaggeration to say that Azusa and the rest are able to live their laid-back lives thanks to you!

All right. If there is a next time, let's meet then!

Going out and swinging by the garbage dump site where I hit on the title again,

*Kisetsu Morita*

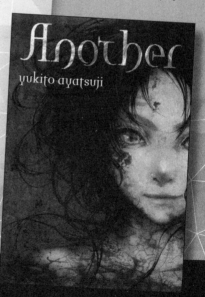